A fascinating space fantasy from Roger Elwood

"The Wandering... may be Elwood's most fascinating work thus far."

Harold Lindsell

In *The Wandering*, Neshi, an elite Tech Detective, uncovers his government's sinister plot to create a new race of people. When the Natasians realize he is aware of their evil plan, Neshi is exiled from his home planet forever.

While wandering through space, Neshi sees chilling evidence of the Natasians' influence throughout the galaxy. Planet after planet lies in decay, their civilizations destroyed by diabolical forces. Neshi eventually lands on Nede, where there is no war, disease, or crime. Hoping that his quest is over, Neshi plans to settle on this idyllic planet. Before long, however, he makes some startling discoveries about his new home, discoveries that cause him to despair. Was there any world that could escape the pervasive power of the Natasians?

BY Roger Elwood

Fiction:

Angelwalk
The Christening
The Wandering
Soaring
Dwellers
Children of the Furor
Fallen Angel
The Sorcerers of Sodom

Nonfiction:

Strange Things Are Happening
Prince of Darkness
People of Destiny
Christian Mothers: Their Joys and Sorrows
The "Innocent" Sins of Everyday Life

SORCERERS
OF SODOM

ROGER ELWOOD

Fleming H. Revell Company
Tarrytown, New York

Library of Congress Cataloging-in-Publication Data

Elwood, Roger.
    The sorcerers of Sodom / Roger Elwood.
        p. cm.
    ISBN 0-8007-5389-5
    I. Title.
    PS3555.L85S6   1991
    813'.54—dc20   90-19947
                                                      CIP

Copyright © 1991 by Roger Elwood
Published by the Fleming H. Revell Company
Tarrytown, New York 10591
Printed in the United States of America

TO Jean and Dwight Hooten
for friendship,
for fellowship,
and the best pork ever

Acknowledgments

One of the people I would most like to acknowledge is Walter Martin, who proved to be a profound influence before his death and whose memory is no less an influence months later. After I had surgery that proved to be significantly more serious than originally estimated, he called me twice in a week to find out how I was feeling. Five days later, he had a fatal heart attack.

Harold Lindsell was also influential in the writing of *The Sorcerers of Sodom*. He is a rock of theological integrity whose friendship has been a blessing over the years. I must also add Warren Wiersbe, whose moments of counsel have been among the most invaluable in my lifetime.

But let me also go back a few years and recognize the

pastor whose gift of teaching honed and shaped my own stance regarding the inerrancy of Scripture and the absolute necessity of salvation through Jesus Christ as Savior and Lord, the Reverend William Conover.

The worst effect of sin is within, and is manifested not in poverty, and in pain, and in bodily defacement, but in . . . the unworthy love, the low ideal, the brutalized and enslaved spirit.

Edwin Hubbell Chapin

Introduction

The Sorcerers of Sodom is a phrase that describes many insidious individuals who are unfortunately gaining an ever-increasing degree of influence in society today, at virtually every level: practicing Satanists. They tend to engage in their awful business undercover, abhorring publicity, preferring to practice loathsome works of darkness in darkness.

"One who practices supernatural power over people and their affairs; witchcraft; black magic. . . ."

That is a standard dictionary's definition of what a sorcerer is; it couldn't be more accurate.

Sorcerers they are, with real power. If Satan and his emissaries had no power and were just paper tigers, then this world would have remained a vibrant, satisfying

Eden. Adam and Eve would never have sinned; disease and pain and death would never have entered into our existence on planet Earth. And, most profoundly, there would have been no need for a sacrifice of Christ on Calvary's cross, followed by His burial and resurrection.

In those ancient biblical times, there were plenty of deceivers and sorcerers. Jesus faced them head-on, never pulling back, risking their vengeance. The danger to Himself didn't matter to our Lord; nothing but the truth did, nothing but the necessity of standing up to the sorcerers and corrupters of His time.

In the 2000 years since then, we have seen endless numbers of their kind pillaging and corrupting, stealing the goods of men and women and corrupting their souls through greed and drugs and humanistic doctrines of the transcendence of man.

The sorcerers of society today—which is a modern Sodom in so many respects—have maintained their power through anonymity. That may be changing, as more truths come to light about their activities. They infiltrate level after level of society's fabric, possible harbingers of the coming reign of the Antichrist.

These sorcerers are the leaders, those involved in the various tributaries of Satanism, the New Age movement, and various cults. But they cannot do it alone. They need help, those who serve as their puppets at film studios, record companies, media companies everywhere, disseminating the doctrines of sex, drugs, hedonism, and a great deal more.

I have met many such individuals over the years. I've talked to them, tried to show them how wrong their life-styles are, only to have them throw back in my face the Scripture that says, "Judge not!" They refuse to listen to what the Lord actually meant by that verse.

The characters in *The Sorcerers of Sodom* are fictitious, but many of the events, circumstances, and infernal practices delineated are factual, based on the most careful research. The potential of fiction to depict the various aspects of biblical prophecy is fascinating and exciting. To a degree, *The Sorcerers of Sodom* is an attempt to interweave the Bible's foretelling of events with a dramatic story of wickedness in high places and that chilling part of Romans that mentions God giving huge numbers of people over to a reprobate mind.

We shouldn't be surprised at what is happening around us today. Biblical prophecy gave these warnings thousands of years ago, and they assume increasing credence as we watch the news on TV and read our newspapers.

There are many readers who will find *The Sorcerers of Sodom* quite unnerving. It is difficult to confront pure evil without finding our sensibilities assaulted. Yet, as Warren Wiersbe commented after reading a previous book of mine, "We need to get from a bumper sticker mentality to a battlefield one. . . . Too many Christians want lullabies."

I pray *The Sorcerers of Sodom* will be an enlightening book, a book that helps prepare its readers for the coming days foretold by the Lord through His inspired prophets—days requiring courage, insight, and all the faith and trust in Jesus Christ that we can muster.

Many have puzzled themselves about the origin of evil. I am content to observe that there is evil, and that there is a way of escape from it, and with this I begin and end.

John Newton

Prologue

They were like lemmings, family after family succumbing to demons eager to possess each one and then dispose of their bodies like rag dolls. . . .

The Reverend Brian Loeffler's hand was shaking as he stood before the bathroom mirror.

"Join us," the old man said. "We have so much to offer."

"No!" he screamed. "I will not! I serve only one Master, the Lord Jesus—"

"Go to hell!" the old man said. "Hell isn't such a bad place, you know. It's a little hot, but the pain can be endured."

He licked his lips.

"You can even learn to enjoy it!"

He was overcome with laughter then, and something else. This man, well into his eighties, suffering from arthritis and *the effects of a stroke, started changing shape, the human outline altering, the skin turning mottled shades of—*

It was not possible to experience an encounter of that sort without being deeply traumatized. The miracle was his very survival of it, any kind of survival at all, even one that left psychological scars that would take years to heal.

Loeffler touched a few vagrant strands dangling down from an ample head of hair that had been turned white.

A year ago, he thought, *it was pitch black. A year ago, I slept in the same bed each night.*

He fought back some tears then.

Marianne, you used to like to run your fingers through my hair when it was wet. . . .

At such a moment of reflection, sweet memories colliding with the ugly and gruesome one, he realized he was relieved his wife had died of leukemia a few years before.

Praise God that she never saw the horror.

He ran his fingers over his face, noting the paleness of his skin, the bloodshot eyes, the ever-increasing wrinkles.

Lord, why do I feel so ancient? And look it?

Loeffler was only in his late thirties, but with his hair the way it was, he gave anyone who met him the distinct impression of more years than that. The hair, yes, but also the seemingly permanent dark circles under his eyes, the—

Turning away from the mirror in resignation, he sighed with a touch of real weariness.

"Lord," he said out loud, "I'm glad to be alive, but there are times when I wonder if it would have been better if I had died in Providence Junction."

The satanic nightmare had begun with seeming innocence. A few teenagers thought it would be fun to hold Ouija board parties every so often. Elsewhere in the town, adults had dabbled in mail-order astrology, and tarot card games had replaced poker and canasta.

It took months. Satan's intrusion started slowly. But it ended one afternoon in the spring of that year with scores of the citizens of Providence Junction dying in the middle of the town square. The mayor. The police chief. Town council members. Providence Junction's librarian. Some nurses and doctors from the local clinic. And a group of teenagers—the town's smartest, most attractive—the ones with the brightest futures ahead of them.

Loeffler started back toward the bedroom, looking around at the unfamiliar furniture, the cheap lithographs surrounded by plastic frames, the loud air conditioner.

How many of these places he had seen in the past year. But when your wife was dead, your town had been destroyed, and most of your friends were either in sanitariums or buried in a common grave, no place can seem like home again. You either go on, make do with the circumstances, or become a hermit and isolate yourself altogether.

Though he was a Baptist clergyman, the notion of shucking everything and joining perhaps a group of Catholic monks in a place of grand and total solitude crossed his mind. *Well,* he thought, *at least they have some degree of control in a material sense. They construct the parameters of their world and stay within it, blocking out virtually everything else.*

Loeffler knew well enough all the standard evangelical admonitions against the necessity of such a life, yet the existence of a monk had seemed, in those early tragic days, truly appealing. For what he had learned from a theological perspective didn't always apply to what was rooted in deep emotion, although these considerations must never be in opposition. While becoming a monk may not have been essential, indeed was *not* essential to his salvation, it could be another matter altogether in terms of his psychological well-being.

He had gone so far as to visit a monastery in a secluded section of the Rocky Mountains near Denver, Colorado. After studying what was available in pamphlet and other forms, he came to the conclusion that the theology of that particular order seemed less antagonistic to his Protestantism than he had supposed, and he looked forward to spending time with its members.

Setting up the stay proved not at all awkward. Apparently the entire group of monks had been following the case of Providence Junction with great interest.

"We would be pleased to have you spend some time with us," Father Petroni told him over the phone. "You are well known among my brothers in this order."

"There is much that I would like to discuss with you," Loeffler remarked. "But even more, it will be wonderful just to separate myself from the rest of the world for a while."

"That is the whole basis for our existence," the other man said. "It is true that Scripture tells us to be in the world, yet we are also told not to be *of* the world. What choice do we make when the world threatens to drag us down into its maw and destroy our emotions, our minds, even our bodies. True, our souls are untouchable, but what about the rest of us?"

Loeffler thanked him and hung up.

He was staying at another minister's house at that point. It was a good transition for him; later, he would move from motel to motel as his speaking schedule became increasingly jammed with commitments.

He had been resting in bed as he made that phone call. Now he stood, walked to the window at the opposite end of the room, and looked outside.

Marianne, he thought as he saw some children playing in the street. *How much you wanted to be a mother. . . .*

He turned away and closed his eyes, thinking of his wife as he had done so often since leaving what used to be Providence Junction but ended up as a smoldering pile of useless ash, much more than bodies buried underneath.

*   *   *

For long hours he would talk to the monks about evil.

"It was visible," he said, anguish written across his face. "It was a living reality that I could face on a finite level, that I could see and touch and—"

They were sitting at a rectangular table after having eaten a dinner comprised of chick-pea soup, stuffed acorn squash, mimosa salad, and pumpkin pea sauce.

Loeffler was feeling free to give of himself to the dozen men at the table with him.

"I had never known of evil in that way before," he confessed.

"For you, it was wrapped in a theological shroud, and not at all personal," Father Petroni offered.

"Exactly," Loeffler agreed. "That was exactly it."

"We can offer a thousand sermons, yet evil remains abstract," the monk commented. "That is, I think, one of Satan's cleverest devices, to get us to view evil from, say, a distance, to think of it in, say, eschatological terms, and discuss it as almost an intellectual exercise."

"Are you saying that Satan hesitates to reveal himself in what might be called cold, hard reality?"

"I think so, Reverend Loeffler. He holds back as much as possible, preferring to manifest his influence in subtler ways that are often more devastating."

"But why does he *ever* materialize, as it were?"

"It is when final victory in a given circumstance is within his grasp. His ego can no longer allow him to work through his puppets, human or demonic. He and he alone must assume center stage and have all eyes directed at himself."

"Have you been . . . face-to-face with the demonic here?" Loeffler asked.

"We have," Father Petroni acknowledged. "Where there is great effort to resist him, he is certain to attack as strongly as he can."

Another monk, Father Capensati, added, "We have witnessed events so bizarre that were we to tell the media, we would be branded religious schizophrenics."

"Events?" Loeffler asked. "Can you give me an example?"

And Father Capensati did just that.

It was large, this shape, large and ferocious, with leathery wings and a face of death, dark and unholy and reeking of lost souls in hell. . . .

"We all saw it," Father Capensati told him. "It was standing there just beyond the wall that surrounds us."

"It did not try to enter?" Loeffler asked.

"No, it did not. As soon as we saw it, we banded together and began offering up prayer to Almighty God, and then it was gone."

"Were there other occasions?"

"Yes, but sir, we need to keep our minds trained on Jesus Christ, not His adversary."

Father Petroni had been observing Loeffler. After Father Capensati had finished, he commented, "Reverend Loeffler, you are so very troubled."

"Yes, I am. My town went up in a blaze all around me. And I may have helped to light the fire."

"Can we be of service?"

"Just talking about it would help."

"Then we will spend as much time as you need."

And they did, they truly did. By the time Loeffler had given them the details of what had happened, it was morning, but they had listened to every word about how possessed citizens of Providence Junction had ended up worshiping something spit up from the bowels of Hades, an entity as loathsome as the ancient Medusa, sent by Satan himself.

SORCERERS OF SODOM

1

Following the destruction of Providence Junction, Brian Loeffler had traveled from town to town, giving seminars about Satan and the occult or acting as guest lecturer at Christian colleges. The deacons at the church to which he had gone as pastor after Providence Junction were sympathetic when he came to them and admitted that he was not ready for the responsibility of a regular pastorate. They continued to collect his messages and his mail; technically he was on a leave of absence, but no one, not even Loeffler himself, knew when or if he would return to his pastorate.

Wherever he went in his wandering, he saw disturbing reminders of the nightmare that had engulfed Providence Junction, a nightmare that showed how real the dangers were when anyone flirted with the occult. He often thought of those enlightening biblical prophecies that spoke profoundly of a chaotic end-times period, one in which immorality would run rampant, children would dishonor their parents, and the work of sorcerers would rise.

Every so often, out of tiredness or a need to connect with the Lord, he would pull over to the side of the road and rest for a bit, his hands shaking.

Sorcerers.

The very term sent chills throughout his body, and he recalled an ominous reference to their occultic practices: "the use of power gained from the assistance . . . of evil spirits." That was unsettling enough, but there was more: "It may be practiced by anyone with the appropriate knowledge, using charms, spells, potions, and the like; whereas witchcraft is considered to result from an inherent mystical power."

Any man, any woman, any child who was interested could use the power of sorcery for any purpose! He thought of the havoc this could unleash. The danger was not so much to believers, for the Holy Spirit had promised them defenses against the evil one. The danger was from experienced sorcerers commanding demonic power against people who had "no time" for Christ, for the Bible, or for God.

But Loeffler knew that he shouldn't be surprised by this. The Bible was explicit about a rise in such practices during the so-called end time. He knew that he was seeing more and more of what God's prophets had foretold through the wisdom and the vision He had bestowed upon them. With his biblical training and insights, how could he think otherwise about the events unfolding around the world, the increased corruption and perversion, the blasphemies that seemed to take place almost daily?

When Loeffler had been in Providence Junction, he had hoped the devastation there was an isolated phenomenon, that, as terrible as it had been, it would not happen again in other places. But in the year since, he had witnessed a significant speeding up of satanic efforts to seduce countless numbers of people by a substitution of demonically inspired "doctrines" for that which was from God Himself.

Now he was in a town in Kansas, one that had seen an upsurge in satanic activity. A group of church leaders had gotten together and sponsored his trip there. He had been gracious and encouraging and agreed to appear, but he was beginning to wonder if he had the strength to go on much longer.

"I only have so much energy, so much stamina," he said as he slipped to his knees. "Lord, I don't know how I can go on much longer."

He sensed the fringes of burnout, sensed the possibility that he was perilously close to it, but he also knew that this could be yet another satanic deception. As he prepared for this lecture, he wondered if he was accomplishing anything besides his own destruction.

Loeffler decided to walk to the church since the evening was so mild; he needed only his suit jacket.

This was a pleasant midwestern town, like so many others he had visited. People said hello as they walked by, there was not much traffic, and the air was clean. He stopped for a moment, breathing it in, enjoying the feel of it against his lungs, then made his way toward the church.

There was a small park in the center of town. He saw a teenage couple, sitting on one of the benches, kissing quite passionately.

He thought of Marianne, beloved Marianne, now dead just three years, thought of their own dates, then the wedding ceremony, their honeymoon in Hawaii on the island of Maui, and the dozen years they had spent as husband and wife. Though not blessed with children, they had had the closest, most satisfying marriage imaginable.

And then you left, he whispered softly to himself. *We both prayed; we had prayer chains going throughout the congregation; we all begged God to spare your life. But He chose to take you. I had to face the nightmare alone.*

Again, for perhaps the hundredth time, he regretted not having her by his side, giving him strength, but soon felt relieved that she hadn't been there to—

"I don't know what I would have done if any of *them* had gotten hold of you," he said out loud, a bit startled that he had done so.

"What was that, sir?"

An elderly woman walking her very large collie stopped for a moment, thinking he had intended to address her.

"Nothing, ma'am," he said, blushing.

She looked at him somewhat doubtfully, then continued on.

Them. . . .

Men and women he had known for years, people he considered friends, were turned into demon-possessed automatons, enslaved to the Arch Deceiver. He believed that redeemed believers could not be indwelt by the forces of darkness, so it must have been that they had been playing a game over the years, professing faith in Christ but none of it more than easy talk, none of it coming from the very center of their souls.

A charade, he told himself, careful not to do so audibly this time. *They went to church, they heard my sermons, then returned to personal lives unaffected by the truths I might have dispensed from the pulpit.*

He approached a cemetery adjacent to the church, paused, went inside, walked among the headstones for a few minutes.

How many times I visited your grave, beloved, he thought. *How many times did I kneel on the ground and weep, the loneliness washing over me.*

He heard choral music coming from the church and bowed his head briefly.

The words, Lord. I need Your help, blessed One. Give me

something to tell them, to help them, to give them a warning they will heed.

The church was medium sized, built like an amphitheater, with Spanish architecture and the best acoustics he had encountered since leaving Providence Junction. Several hundred people were sitting in well-padded pews, looking up at the podium as he stood after being introduced by Pastor Warren Halsey, a burly former football player in his late forties.

Loeffler's palms were sweaty. Even after spending much of his adult life in some public forum, speaking before a group still made him nervous until he had been at it for a few minutes and warmed up sufficiently. Still, tonight's tingle of apprehension seemed stronger than his normal case of butterflies.

"My brothers and sisters in Christ, I am happy to be here," he began. "What I have to say isn't cheerful or pleasant but rather alarming. We are in a dangerous period, a period in which satanic activity is increasing and the specter of demonic—"

"Who do you think you are, anyway?" a voice called from the back.

A teenage boy stood and crossed over to the center aisle.

"You failed with your own church!" he said as he walked down the aisle toward the podium. "Why should we listen to you?"

"What's your name, son?" Loeffler asked, trying to appear calm.

"Shawn."

The boy was in front of Loeffler now, looking up at the raised podium. "We can't fight the forces of darkness," he said. "We're too weak."

"You're right," Loeffler agreed. "*We* are too weak." Shawn seemed surprised.

"But we *can* do all things through Christ who strengthens us," Loeffler continued.

"Where was Christ when you lived in Providence Junction?"

"I had turned away from Him. I admit it. I realized what was wrong, but it was too late to do any good."

Shawn started laughing as he shouted, "Hypocrite! Weakling!"

The church's pastor got to his feet and approached the teenager. "Shawn, you must stop this," he said. "I don't know what's gotten—"

"—into me?" Shawn finished the sentence for him. "That's what you were going to say, isn't it?" He grabbed the front of the muscle shirt he wore.

"Well, I'll show you!" he shrieked as he tore it open, revealing a pentagram that had been tattooed on his chest. "This is the only source of power and eternal life that means anything."

Shawn pointed to the large cross anchored to the center of the platform where Loeffler stood.

"Not that ridiculous symbol of defeat!"

Loeffler came out from behind the podium. "The cross signals death *and* resurrection," he said.

"It's a toy for weak minds and enslaved spirits."

"Satan is the one who enslaves, Shawn."

"Satan is my *liberator!*" Shawn pulled a revolver from a pocket of his leather jacket.

The pastor stepped back reflexively.

"I can use this on anyone I want. It gives me the power of life and death. For a couple of hundred dollars, anyone can have this power. Anyone can point the barrel at someone else and blow him away."

He turned to the pastor and fired one shot. The man was flung backward by the force of it.

People began screaming in panic, getting up from the pews, and starting to run in every direction.

"No!" Shawn shouted at them. "Nobody moves. I shoot anybody who does."

Loeffler jumped off the platform and stood only a few feet from the teenager, his hand extended in front of him. There was no fear or anger on his face—only pity and forgiveness.

"Give me the gun, Shawn. Christ died for you, too."

For a moment Shawn froze where he stood. Then his face reddened as he started to weep.

"Too late!" Shawn said, then suddenly pressed the barrel of the gun to his own temple and pulled the trigger.

How much like another youngster seemed . . . the nine-year-old boy who had become addicted to drugs because they made contact with certain spirits easier.

"I can get them anytime I want," the boy had told him. "Five minutes from now, I can be high."

They were sitting in an empty office at the school the nine-year-old attended—yet he didn't have to leave the grounds to buy crack, marijuana, heroin!

"And it helps, it helps, it helps me when I drink the blood," the boy added.

"The blood?"

"Yeah. From dogs, cats, you know. I drank it, like lemonade."

He was laughing then, for the moment obviously enjoying the memories.

It was all Loeffler could do to control himself, to stop from reaching out and shaking the boy!

Loeffler rode in the ambulance with Pastor Halsey, who had been hit in the shoulder and lost a fair amount of blood but would definitely survive.

"One of our finest young men," Halsey said, his voice weak. "I had no idea."

"Parents and pastors often don't," Brian told him.

"But how could I not have seen *something*?"

"I noticed you have a lot of activity at church."

"It's a well-rounded church."

"Warren, I counted more than twenty events in one week!" Loeffler went on to tell Halsey about his own experiences in Providence Junction. "Activity is often a facade. Activity can replace quiet moments of prayer and can become Satan's device to distract us from what really matters. It is a mistake to construe activity as an indication of real, deep-down accomplishment."

Perhaps Halsey ordinarily would have been offended at such a criticism, but he had just come undeniably face-to-face with one of the fruits of his approach.

"Are you saying that Shawn fell through the cracks?" he asked.

"When there is too much activity, it isn't unusual for more than one individual to be left out. Maybe Shawn was turned off by the church socials, the afternoon teas, the volleyball games, the picnics, all the rest. He was hungering for something, Warren."

"And I starved him into trying to get whatever he needed from Satan!" Halsey groaned. "I wonder how many more are on the verge of doing what he did."

Loeffler had no answer.

2

Loeffler knew he had to get away, to separate himself from his mission for a bit, and when this need became apparent, he felt guilty. He felt that it signaled weakness, as though he were announcing to God that perhaps he should do something else, maybe return to a cozy pastorate.

But where do I go? he asked himself. *Where can I hope to recharge my energy?*

His late wife and he had spent some vacation time in an isolated spot near Colorado Springs at a retreat owned by a Christian organization.

Too many memories, he decided.

He made that decision in a southwestern luncheonette while looking out at the highway, which was not well traveled. The few customers inside seemed as weary as the solitary waitress. He closed his eyes for a minute.

"You seem tired," he said as she was pouring some coffee.

"I am," she replied.

"So it gets busier than this?"

"That's not why I'm tired, sir."

"Sorry. I didn't mean to pry."

"That's all right."

She hesitated a moment.

"You're a minister, aren't you?" she asked.

"Yes, I am. How did you know?"

"Nobody else would put a Bible on top of the table, as you've done."

She seemed to be ready to say something else.

"Ma'am, can I help you?" Loeffler asked.

"I'm tired of life," she said. "I'm tired of living. I have nothing to live for. That doesn't mean I'm thinking of suicide because I'm not. I just want something to do. Being a waitress can take you only so far."

"So far? Money, you mean?"

"More than that, sir. Some kind of goal."

"A mission?"

"Something like that."

"I hope you discover what it should be."

"Pray for me, please."

"I will."

Loeffler leaned back against the booth after she had gone to the kitchen.

She needs a mission and doesn't have one. Having a mission would give her life a sense of real meaning.

He closed his eyes again.

I have a mission also but wonder if I can keep on with it any longer.

"Sir, are you all right?" a voice asked.

He opened his eyes and smiled at the waitress.

"Yes. Just a little tired," he told her.

"Do you mind if I say something?" she asked. "I really feel I have to tell you this."

"Not at all. Go ahead."

"You're struggling over a problem, aren't you?"

"Yes."

She looked down at Loeffler's Bible.

"Don't give up, pastor. You've got a way about you. Take some time off, but don't let the devil make you throw in the towel."

Loeffler was astonished. He was sure he looked tired, but how had she known his weariness went deeper than that?

One of the other customers was becoming impatient. The waitress apologized and turned away, leaving Loeffler smiling. God had settled the matter in His own way, and a tired minister was going on vacation, memories or not.

He drove for three days and spent the next week at

the retreat, confronting memories of the time Marianne and he had shared, a happier time that he never wanted to forget.

Soon he felt better, his mind as well as his body rested, losing the feeling of weariness and pointlessness that had dogged him for so long. He walked along the rugged mountain trails for hours at a time, stopping every so often to sit on a stone or at the side of the road to open his Bible and seek the guidance he needed.

On his final day at the retreat, he received a phone call.

The familiar voice carried a note of apprehension.

"I really do need your insights, Brian," said Judson McClane. "You may not have all the answers, but what you've been through over the past year could be of great help."

Loeffler was sitting by his bed in the ninety-year-old castle that housed guests at the retreat. His speakers' bureau always had his complete itinerary and generally knew how to get in touch with him on a moment's notice.

"But aren't there others with far more wisdom, Judson?"

"Yes, but . . ."

"Do you think your problem might be demonically based?"

"I'm afraid so. We've found only one bit of evidence as such, though."

"May I guess what it was?" Loeffler described a wood carving, faintly Aztec in appearance.

"Exactly!" McClane acknowledged. "You're familiar with it?"

"Intimately," Loeffler assured him.

He and Judson McClane had been friends since seminary days. McClane was one of the first individuals Loeffler had talked with since leaving Providence Junction after the holocaust there, but they had lost contact since then. Nearly five years before, McClane had been appointed chancellor of Four Gospels Christian College on the beachfront outskirts of Hollywood, California.

"What a blessing it was to come here," McClane told him on the telephone. "The students seemed on fire for Christ. The academic program was among the best in the country. And the whole physical environment seemed like a piece of a modern-day Eden. You'll see what I mean when you get here."

"But what's happened?" Brian asked.

"Grades started to fall, discipline deteriorated noticeably, and drug use showed up." McClane hesitated, then continued. "Four Gospels was once different from its secular counterparts, but now the changes here are beginning to erode that difference, Brian."

Loeffler managed to drag more facts out of McClane, who seemed reluctant to voice them.

"All right, Brian," McClane sighed. "You've not lost your touch, my friend."

Animals.

Piles of them blocking the main thoroughfare into Four Gospels.

It happened in the middle of the night.

Dozens of dogs, cats, birds, even spider monkeys.

All dead!

Many had been that way for some time. The stench was overpowering.

For days after the incident, the significance of it was given lively debate. One or two dead animals thrown onto Four Gospels property would have been curious indeed, but not fifty!

"Demonic influence is on the rise everywhere," Loeffler offered. "But perhaps you're in some kind of vortex there."

"I suspect so, Brian." McClane was silent briefly, then added, "Don't you feel Armageddon coming?"

He knew immediately what his friend meant. "Yes, I do, faster and faster. It's a cliché, I know, but I can almost feel it in the air and taste it in my mouth."

"Praise God for you, Brian. Anytime, of course, but especially right now. I was beginning to wonder if my paranoid fantasies were taking over. The fact that the Tribulation hasn't occurred doesn't change my apprehension." He paused for a second or two, then continued. "There's more involved out here that I would rather tell you in person. Just think about this in the meantime. Biblical prophecy, as you know, indicates that in the days prior to the appearance of the Antichrist, there will be . . . ."

"The phenomena of demons led by their master seeking whom they may entrap and therefore devour," Loeffler offered.

"Exactly. But there's something else, Brian."

"What's that?"

"One of the more prominent aspects of the prophecy. I mean, wickedness in high places."

"What are you saying, Judson?"

"Here, Brian: in the police department, in county government. But, please, let's not talk any more about it by phone."

After the connection had been broken, Loeffler started going through his Bible, concentrating on the prophetic portions. Soon he was well into the passages in the Book of Revelation that dealt with the Four Horsemen of the Apocalypse. "Warfare, famine, earthquakes, false religions and messiahs," he mused out loud.

Be not deceived.

He sighed as he read those three simple yet powerful words, his hands instinctively gripping the Bible more tightly.

Apparently, Lord, You think I'm ready for another one.

Brian Loeffler wished he was sure of that.

The drive to California was a long one. Loeffler had to pass through many small desert towns, and one of them was on an Indian reservation.

He saw near poverty there—little children with dirt-smudged faces, clothes that were torn and soiled.

A little boy sitting beside the road caught his attention as he drove slowly by. Ordinarily he wouldn't have stopped, but there was something about this child, something so sad that Loeffler knew he had no alternative but to see what was wrong. He stopped his car a hundred yards or so away, got out, and walked slowly back toward the child.

The boy looked up at him, tears in his eyes.

"Why are you so sad?" Loeffler asked as he bent down. He had the urge to wrap the boy in his arms and comfort him but resisted it. There was a sense of dignity in the child that he would not patronize.

"I'm hungry."

"Where can I get you something to eat?"

The little boy shook his head.

"No work no more," he said.

"What do you mean?"

The boy held up something that had been nestled in his lap.

A small wood carving.

Loeffler bolted to his feet and backed away, startled. It was just like the Aztec devil god carvings in Providence Junction a year earlier! Suddenly he could move no farther, having backed into a solid obstacle of hard flesh. He turned around and saw a tall, very broad Indian in his late thirties standing there, looking at him.

"What is there about my son that disturbs you?" the man dressed in a T-shirt and tattered jeans asked with a note of suspicion.

44

Loeffler was more than a little embarrassed.

"It was that carving," he said, his face red.

"Such a simple piece of wood stirs you so?"

"It's a very long story."

"I have some time. I have nothing but time."

The three of them walked back toward several adobe huts some distance from the road.

Loeffler glanced around at the village, saw old women just standing or sitting, looking into space, their faces deeply lined; smelled the odor that always came when waste disposal was inadequate; saw proud men wearing rags; saw the shame that was eating away at them on their faces.

"I would offer you something to eat," the man said as they entered his home, which was essentially nothing more than an adobe hut with bare wood furniture and an ancient, rather noisy refrigerator, "but my son and I have very little ourselves. I am afraid I can give you only some juice."

"I do not drink alcohol," Loeffler said as politely as possible.

"I do not serve it. This is unfermented."

Loeffler blushed again, ashamed of the way he had jumped to the wrong conclusion.

"My name is Henry Running Stream. Yours?"

"Brian Loeffler."

"Now tell me why that wood carving upsets you so."

Loeffler recounted the story of Providence Junction

and how the same carving had been a focal point for concentration on demonic forces.

"It is interesting, what you say," Running Stream told him. "I had another son. His name was River Brooks. He left many moons ago. I have not heard from him since. That carving was in his room. My little boy won't let it out of his sight."

The Indian closed his eyes for a moment, then opened them, a sigh of great weariness coursing through his body.

"It is difficult for me. My whole life has been filled with images of wood and stone and soil, and gods of wind and sun and moon and rain."

"And here I am, suggesting that that little carving may be evil."

Running Stream looked at him.

"How well you sense what I am trying to say."

Running Stream stood and walked to the doorway of the hut, stirring up little puffs of dust from the dirt floor.

"We have only the natural things," he said. "It is not surprising that those natural things have become our gods." He bowed his head briefly. "Our medicine men are little different from the witch doctors of Africa. Brian Loeffler, we *are* pagans. We have been for a very long time."

"Your son—River Brooks?"

"Yes?"

"How much did his behavior change after he got the carving?"

"A great deal. He's a singer. He dreamed of a career in the music business, dreamed of earning a lot of money and taking us with him to live in a mansion. That was at the beginning. Later, he talked only of the money."

"You speak as though you will never see him again."

"I may not. He has disappeared. No one knows where he is."

Loeffler cleared his throat. The interior of this man's home was quite dusty.

"Why don't you get rid of the carving?" he asked.

Running Stream turned from the doorway and walked over to a large leather-covered chest at the opposite side of the room. He lifted the lid and asked Loeffler to look inside. There were a dozen or more carvings, each one different in size and detail.

"Which one should I get rid of first, Brian Loeffler?" Running Stream asked pointedly.

He picked up one carving after another.

"This one represents the god of our corn crop. This one is the god of rain."

There was a separate god for a separate purpose: gods for crops, for weather, for health, for everything.

"You have an all-purpose deity," Running Stream said. "We don't have that luxury. Our prayers are far more complicated."

"I would like to think that someday you—" Loeffler started to say.

He didn't finish the sentence. The sound of screeching tires interrupted him, and the two of them rushed outside.

Bored by their conversation, the little boy had wandered back outside and was crying as he stood beside the road. Racing ahead was a car leaving a trail of dust behind it.

"They don't care," Running Stream said as he knelt and hugged his boy. "They can run over any of us, and it doesn't matter. To them, we're like that dirty cloud that follows them."

Loeffler wished he had the right words, wished he could bring up some handy verse from Scripture. But he also knew that Running Stream's emotions would have gotten in the way, so he simply bent down beside the two of them and put his arms around them.

When they finally stood, Running Stream looked at Loeffler curiously.

"There are tears on your cheeks," he said.

"Because I feel your pain."

Running Stream took his son back to their home and then returned.

"Do you understand how little the white man weeps for us?" he asked pointedly.

"I can imagine that it hasn't been very much."

"You may be only the second I can remember."

A minute or two passed.

Loeffler thought of the stereotypes perpetrated by the entertainment industry through sixty years of filmmaking and television. Indians were invariably the villains rising up against the innocent white man.

How conveniently such images ignored the atrocities committed by white settlers and battalions of soldiers. Often whole villages were wiped out. There were documented cases of near genocide that didn't stop at women and children, soldiers proudly displaying babies stuck on the ends of their swords or bayonets!

"I have to be going now," Loeffler said finally. "I am heading toward Hollywood."

"Ah, yes," Running Stream said, scratching his chin, "a place where they know much about idols, is it not, sir?"

Loeffler had to agree.

"Do you think River is there?" he asked the other man.

Running Stream nodded.

"I do," he said. "You are probably wondering why I never went to see him."

"That's true," Loeffler admitted.

"My son made it clear that he no longer wanted to recognize me, his brother, this tribe."

Running Stream walked with Loeffler back to the minister's car.

"You must think of me harshly," the Indian said.

"Not at all!" Loeffler protested, not wanting to leave the man with that kind of impression. "I know more than a little about the history of native Americans over the past hundred years."

"Like Wounded Knee?"

"Yes, like Wounded Knee."

The infamous scene of what was a final spasm of violence when, on October 29, 1890—just four days after Christmas!—U.S. cavalrymen massacred two hundred Oglala Sioux, virtually an entire village, at Wounded Knee, South Dakota.

Running Stream interrupted Loeffler's thoughts. "That is on a level where few would disagree with you, except perhaps the Klu Klux Klan. However, please be honest with yourself: don't you consider me a victim of delusion, a heathen under the sway of demonic spirits?"

Loeffler's shoulders slumped.

"I cannot blame you, Brian Loeffler," Running Stream said. "You are the product of your culture."

He reached out and put his hands on Loeffler's shoulders.

"But then so am I a product of mine. My ancestry may go back to the time of the Aztecs who originated that little carving. We have lived centuries with our idols. Can you expect us to so easily sweep them aside?"

Loeffler admitted that Running Stream had a point.

"I can only hope that you, a decent man, will see the truth."

"Assuming that I haven't seen it already?"

Running Stream paused very briefly and then spoke of an Indian named George P. Lee.

"Have you heard of him?" he asked.

Loeffler nodded.

"I admire him in some ways."

"How so?"

"George and I are distant cousins, Brian Loeffler. When he became a Mormon, I wished him well but . . . ."

"But what?" Loeffler asked.

"Somehow I knew he wouldn't be happy."

"Because you sensed the falsity of the Mormon belief system, is that it?"

"Again you surprise me," Running Stream admitted.

"I do know something about the matter. George P. Lee became the first major Mormon leader in forty-six years to be excommunicated by the hierarchy."

"That is right. He accused the Mormons of spiritually slaughtering his people, of destroying them for all eternity."

"Because he had become convinced that clinging to Mormonism would only lead them directly to hell."

Running Stream looked at the minister directly.

"One of the comments he made after the excommunication was, 'It got to the point where I had to follow them or Jesus Christ, and I chose to follow Jesus Christ.' "

"The Man you admire?"

"The Man I admire very much, Brian Loeffler."

Loeffler didn't press the matter any further but simply wrote down the name of Four Gospels Christian College, and the phone number.

"I'll be there for a few days," he said, handing the sheet of paper to the other man. "Call me if you want to talk."

They shook hands. Loeffler got back into the car and drove off, realizing that the encounter would stay with him for a long, long time.

3

Evil . . . is a fact not to be explained away, but to be accepted; and accepted not to be endured, but to be conquered. It is a challenge neither to our reason nor to our patience, but to our courage.
John Haynes Holmes

Tired and hungry, with several hours of travel still ahead of him, Brian Loeffler pulled into a diner and sat at the counter. A minute or so later, a middle-aged, rather plump waitress came to take his order.

He noticed that she seemed nervous.

"Are you all right?" he asked.

"Yes, sir, just fine," she replied unconvincingly.

He told her what he wanted, and she turned away

from the counter, but in doing so, she knocked a metal napkin holder on the floor. After picking it up and putting it back, she looked at Loeffler. "It's him," she said, nodding to her right.

Loeffler turned slowly and saw a man dressed in an army camouflage outfit.

"He just sits there, humming to himself," she said.

"What's wrong with that?"

"It's like a chant or something—really eerie."

Loeffler strained his ears, trying to hear the man above the conversations of other customers.

The man stood and walked to the nearby men's room.

"He has something on the table—a drawing. He keeps looking at it." She glanced at the Bible Loeffler had placed on the counter when he first sat down. "I'm telling you this because I'm a believer, like you."

"Then why are you so afraid?"

She frowned. "I love my Lord but fear my destroyer."

Loeffler nodded.

The waitress's eyes widened a bit.

Loeffler glanced back.

The man had returned to his table.

Several minutes passed. Loeffler was eating chicken fried steak and green beans when he heard an argument in progress.

The man in army garb had grabbed the waitress, and she was trying to pull away from him.

A trucker who must have weighed three hundred pounds stood and hurried over to the two of them.

"Leave her alone!" he demanded.

The other man stood. He was outweighed by perhaps a hundred pounds, but after shoving the waitress to one side, he hit the trucker in the stomach with such force that the man collapsed like a very large balloon and tumbled halfway down the length of the diner.

Dazed but angrier than ever, the trucker got to his feet and lunged for the other man.

This time, the trucker was picked up and thrown through the tinted front window of the diner, shattering glass in a dozen directions.

Loeffler had seen something like this happen with a teenager on PCP, a drug that imparted a temporary, startling burst of strength.

After disposing of the trucker, the man in army garb turned and faced the other customers. Veins bulged in his forehead; his eyes were wide. Saliva dripped out of the corners of his open mouth. And then he went totally berserk.

The malevolence of his actions didn't take Loeffler totally by surprise, since he had encountered much demonically inspired behavior, but the others in the diner were sent into mass panic. In a dash for the front entrance, one of the customers knocked Loeffler down. As he fell, he hit his head on the edge of the counter and ended up on the floor, nearly trampled by the other customers.

Loeffler struggled to get to his feet, fighting back a

threatening wave of unconsciousness. His vision blurred. People were screaming and crying in pain.

Suddenly the man stood before him. "Brave or stupid you must be!" he said, grabbing Loeffler by the neck.

Then the man noticed the Bible still on top of the counter. "What's *that* doing here?" he growled.

For an instant his grip loosened, and Loeffler managed to break away, grabbing his Bible. "You know what's in here, don't you?" he said. "It's a book that ends in doom for your master. Biblical prophecy is clear! All the demons . . ."

The man's eyes widened as flecks of foam appeared on the edges of his lips.

". . . will join him in the lake of fire," Loeffler continued, "for all eternity, the punishment for—"

The man started ripping at his clothes and spouting obscenities that made Loeffler cringe, even though he thought he had heard every possible variation since he had left Providence Junction.

And then suddenly the man stopped, reaching out for the Bible, tears flowing down his cheeks. "Please, sir. Let me hold it but for a moment," the man whispered.

Loeffler handed the Bible to him, and he started leafing through the pages, shudders visibly gripping his body.

"All lies," he said, reverting back to anger. Then, "God knows I don't *want* to be like this."

Abruptly demonic control resurged, and he started

ripping the thin pages out in large handfuls, tossing them first to one side, then the other. He stopped once more, looking at the paper littering the floor and at what was left of the Bible.

"Help me, please. Please, please!" he said.

Instantly he began to cough. "Jesus, I need Jesus," he said as he fell to his knees.

Loeffler bent down next to him. "Yes! Jesus! You *do* need Jesus. As your Savior but also your Lord. The Holy Spirit will—"

The man's face contorted with laughter. "I don't need *anyone*."

Suddenly he was on top of Loeffler, choking him. Foaming saliva dripped onto the minister's forehead and cheeks. And the odors—sweat and urine—a stench that seemed to reek from every pore of the man!

Loeffler was dizzy, about to lose consciousness.

"I claim the protection of Christ's shed blood," he managed to whisper.

The man released Loeffler and jumped to his feet, looking around at the empty diner.

"The blood?" he said in mock puzzlement. "The blood of the Lamb, as you call it? You—you—" His voice started to sputter, and he began to mumble deliriously.

"The blood!" he shouted. "I can't stand the mention of that holy blood. I see it now, a wave of it ready to surge over me and—"

"And cleanse," Loeffler said, just barely able to stand.

"No!"

"Yes! Cleanse! It does that. It *does!* Hold your hands under the crimson flow. Look up at His holy face."

The man held out his hands, his head tilted toward the ceiling of the diner.

"I see the cross," he shouted. "I see the cross of the Savior." He walked forward a foot or two. "I look up into His glorious face. I—"

Suddenly convulsions tore through his body, as though he had just ingested a poison that was causing his entire system to rebel in ghastly pain.

"O Jesus," he whimpered. "O Lord Jesus!"

He started sobbing and fell into Loeffler's arms.

Loeffler guided him to one of the booths, and they sat down.

"Something stood in front of me a moment ago," the man managed to say. "Something awful. It said terrible things—you know—things that were evil. It would not let me past at first, but I threw it aside, and then I could stand before Jesus. Sweet, sweet Jesus."

Minutes later, state troopers had arrived and were starting to lead him to a squad car.

He turned and looked at Loeffler.

"Their kind didn't want you to continue on ahead. They fear you. I was supposed to stop you."

"Fear me?"

"Where you are going, they have much control. They don't want any of it ripped from them."

Loeffler thanked him.

An officer approached the minister.

"Are you all right, sir?"

Loeffler nodded.

"What a nut!" the officer exclaimed, shaking his head, after the man had gotten into the car.

"Much more than that," Loeffler told him. "Much more than that."

4

Loeffler was approaching Hollywood.

A smoggy mist blanketed the community to his right, stinging his eyes and making them water a bit. To his left was the San Fernando Valley.

As he left the Hollywood Freeway, he passed the famed Hollywood Bowl, then turned right onto Sunset Boulevard.

He passed the Chateau Marmont, where John Belushi died of a drug overdose. Nearby was the Playboy Building, and a block or two west, he saw two prostitutes trying to attract customers.

Then he noticed the billboards. One presented a photograph of a blonde woman with large breasts accentuated by a tight-fitting sweater; she was looking out at passersby over the top of her sunglasses. Another showed two men holding hands above a headline that read: "We're a civil rights issue—not a moral judgment!"

There were others, all extolling values that were the opposite of Judeo-Christian values, all dedicated to carnality of one stripe or another. Loeffler was eager to get past that section of town.

He entered Beverly Hills, passed homes worth a million dollars, two, three, four million, as high as fifteen million, he was sure. Every lawn was beautifully attended to; Jaguars or Mercedes or BMWs or Rolls-Royces were parked in the driveways.

How many poor families could be helped with just a portion of the extravagance in just a single square mile of this community?

The thought brought a wave of deep sadness.

And when they are dying, and they have not accepted Christ as their Savior and Lord, what will they have left out of all this?

Loeffler finally reached the end of Sunset Boulevard and crossed over to Pacific Coast Highway. The air was clean, laced with ocean scents, the water to his left alternating shades of blue and turquoise, so clear that he was reminded of Hawaii.

He saw teenagers with their surfboards heading toward the beach. A young man, no more than twenty or twenty-one years old, walked dazedly at the side of the road to Loeffler's right. He stumbled, picked himself up, stumbled again.

Loeffler stopped the car and got out, rushing to the youth.

"Do you need help?" he asked.

The young man looked at him and said, "The whole world needs help."

Loeffler grabbed him as he was about to fall, noticing that the veins on one arm were largely collapsed.

"I don't need anything but a clean needle. I don't want to die of AIDS, you know! And some good *stuff*, you know what I mean. I need some stuff."

"I'll get you some medical attention," Loeffler said.

"I don't need that crap," the youth replied, his eyes widening in anger. "I just want to—"

He stopped talking for a moment, looking at Loeffler.

"You're a minister, aren't you?" he asked.

Loeffler nodded.

"It's not my body that's going to hell, sir. It's my soul. I can almost feel those flames on me now. I—"

He started shaking then and fell against Loeffler, who eased him down to the ground.

Just ahead was a public telephone. Loeffler ran to it and dialed 911. After he had given the location as best he could, he went back to the young man, who had curled himself into a fetal position on the gravel-topped ground.

The young man told an intriguing and startling story

then, in spurts, with Loeffler having to fill in the missing pieces.

His name was Arnold Beckerman. He had worked in Hollywood. One day he was invited to a party given by some city officials. It was there that he was introduced to a seemingly endless stream of cocaine.

"The mayor's assistant gave me some," he blurted out. "I liked it. I liked it a lot."

The mayor's assistant! At a party probably sponsored by taxpayers' money!

And it went on from there—more parties, more cocaine, supplemented by other drugs.

"Freebasing was the best. It gave me the quickest hit. Man, I flew to the moon and back!"

Months later, he had a habit. He got a large percentage of his drugs free because he went to the right parties. But the rest he had to pay for himself.

"And then that—that—"

Blood started to drip from his nose, little drops at first, then a large stream of it. Loeffler ran back to his car and got some tissues and then, returning to the youth, he stuffed one up each nostril. In a minute or two the bleeding stopped.

"You were referring to someone," Loeffler said. "What did he do to you?"

"It wasn't what he did," he said. "It was what he wanted to do. I ain't no gay bait, not for anyone, no matter how powerful he is."

Loeffler heard the ambulance's siren. Seconds later it

had pulled up near them. He waited until the young man had been put into the back, and the ambulance had left, before he got into his car and drove away.

He could scarcely wait to get to Four Gospels Christian College.

5

The college grounds encompassed a large expanse of land on the outskirts of a beachfront community, with rolling lawns punctuated by palm trees and lushly colored flower beds. The buildings were Spanish-style, some quite old, others much newer, added over the years of growth enjoyed by the institution.

Loeffler drove up a driveway lined by tall, thin Italian cypress trees that swayed gently as they were caressed by ocean breezes. He sighed as he looked up at the clear sky and smelled the saltwater-tinged air. To his left was a tennis court. To his right, a young man was sitting on a large rock, looking in his direction.

Their gazes met for an instant, then the student

quickly turned his attention to a book he was holding.

Loeffler shrugged his shoulders and continued up the winding road to the college's administration building. After parking, he got out of the car and stood there for a moment, enjoying the openness of the grounds. So many colleges were captives of their environment, surrounded by the cities in which they were located, which meant noise, pollution, and what he dubbed a graffiti mentality.

Not here, he told himself. *Clean and bright and an open target! A kind of scholastic Garden of Eden, ripe for serpentine inroads.*

Young people had been a part of the demonic scheme for decades, ever since the turbulent, protest- and drug-oriented sixties. Then it was Timothy Leary, hippies, college protests, and social revolution. Loeffler remembered those years well, remembered how attractive the notion of absolute freedom was to young people at the time, remembered the havoc brought upon the nation as a result.

He snapped out of his reverie as he pulled up in front of the Spanish-ivy-covered administration building. Then he glanced over his shoulder. That same young man was still there, looking in his direction. Again!

Judson McClane's office was filled with plaques and statues and framed certificates, awards and commendations from educational associations, Christian as well as secular, and more, including photographs of him with noted figures—evangelists, politicians, a few movie stars.

McClane, a former collegiate football player, had lost none of his massive frame and still moved with athletic sureness as he greeted his old friend. "I have something you might recognize," he said as he sat down behind an imposing desk, reached into a desk drawer, and took out something quite familiar to the minister. "Is this what you had in mind when we talked on the phone?" he asked.

Beads of perspiration broke out on Loeffler's forehead. "Yes," he said. "Could we get some fresh air?"

"Certainly. Why don't you tell me as we walk around the campus?"

Loeffler nodded gratefully. Outside, Loeffler told McClane about what had happened earlier that day at the diner.

"Increasingly out in the open," McClane mused.

"Oh, yes," Loeffler agreed. "There is more than a hint in the Bible as to what will happen before our eyes. Prophecy's entire thrust is to point the way. Eighteen months ago," Loeffler said. "That was the first time I had a clue."

"And you couldn't possibly tell before then?" the other man asked, a somewhat incredulous tone in his voice.

Loeffler's shoulders slumped a bit.

"I was blinded by the rosy sermons being swallowed by my congregation," he admitted.

"I know the kind you mean: The way to heaven is paved by dollar bills. Name your car or your mink coat or your diamond ring and claim it, because that is what the Lord wants you to have, brother!"

McClane shivered.

"As seductive as any lie Satan has ever propagated," he said. "It is a constant battle for us here."

McClane waved his arm in front of him.

"Running what we have here is expensive. It is quality education in quality surroundings. But I have to spend nearly as much time as a fund-raiser as I do on my administrative duties."

They talked awhile longer, McClane appreciating Loeffler's candor.

"Obviously what happened did change you, Brian," he observed.

"More than anyone will ever know."

Loeffler sensed someone staring at him. He stopped walking, looked around, and saw the same male student as earlier.

"I noticed him when I arrived," Brian said, nodding in the young man's direction.

"Oh, that's Corey Alderton. He's been anxiously awaiting your arrival."

Loeffler breathed a sigh of relief. He knew he was

slightly paranoid—who wouldn't be after the things he had seen—but was happy to know it was nothing, this time.

"I'll introduce you," McClane said, waving for Corey to come down to them.

The young man walked quickly across the grass to the pathway where Loeffler and McClane stood. A few minutes later, the three of them were sitting on flat rocks at the end of a promontory overlooking the Pacific Ocean, the buildings of the college behind them. An ocean breeze carried with it pungent scents.

"I love it here," Corey was telling them. "I wouldn't want anything to spoil it."

Twenty miles to their left were the outlines of skyscrapers in Los Angeles, a tinted cloud hanging over them.

"In town the air is dirty," he said. "Out here it's so clean."

Just below where they were sitting, surfers carried their boards into the water.

Corey bowed his head in prayer.

"Lord, You've brought us together for a reason. I claim the name of Your Son, Our Savior, in trying to get through the ignorance and confusion that Satan would try to keep wound tightly around us. We want only Your honor and glory."

"I knew someone you would have enjoyed having as a friend," Loeffler remarked, thinking of one of the young people who had resisted Satan back in Providence Junction.

"Bill Maddison?"

Loeffler's eyes widened.

Corey chuckled a bit.

"I've followed everything available about Providence Junction," he admitted.

He took a sheet of brown wrapping paper out of a pocket of his jeans.

"Look at the postmark, sir."

PROVIDENCE JUNCTION, KANSAS
SEPTEMBER 13, 1984

"Where did you get this, Corey?" Loeffler asked, startled.

"My brother." Emotion choked off his voice.

McClane interceded.

"Corey's brother Jason committed suicide toward the end of that year. Grasped tightly in his hand was one of those wood carvings."

"But it's not just the carvings anymore, sir," Corey spoke up. "It's crystals. Some of my high school friends are really into crystalmania. And I know that with some of them, it's going to be just like it was with Jason."

"Would you be willing to tell Reverend Loeffler about River?" McClane asked.

"River?" Loeffler repeated. "Was his full name River Brooks?"

"How did you know?" Corey asked.

"I met his father during the trip here."

"Henry Running Stream?"

"That's right. He told me that his son had left him, his little brother, and the entire tribe behind."

"That's true. But did he say why?"

"Only something about being tired of the old ways."

"That's only part of it, sir."

"But, Corey, how in the world did you ever get to know River Brooks?"

"He was a night-course student here."

"At Four Gospels?"

Corey nodded.

Loeffler was surprised—from an Indian reservation steeped in pantheism and idol worship to a Christian college.

Corey added, "He felt smothered by those old ways and the ceremonies. After a certain point, they made him sick to his stomach. He could sense the demonism inherent in them."

"And so he hungered after something different, something richer and more meaningful?" Loeffler interpolated.

"It seems so, sir."

"But he's not here now. What happened, Corey?"

"He was interested in music. He could write songs,

play several instruments, and had a very good singing voice. Plus, sir, the girls considered him extremely good-looking. All the Hollywood agents he met told him he had the right look and a lot of talent. He left the college, assuring me and his other friends that his faith was strong enough to withstand any of the temptations."

Corey took something else out of his pocket—the headline-splashed cover of one of the supermarket tabloids: "New Singing Sensation River Brooks Disappears."

"What happened to him?" Loeffler asked.

"No way of telling, sir, but he's been missing for weeks now. He'd gotten sidetracked into the occult, which is growing in its influence out here. The start for him was reading some New Age books by that Hollywood columnist."

"I know all about her, Corey," Loeffler assured him. "The Bible isn't exactly silent about her type. But how many have been seduced by her ideas?"

"I can name one, sir."

A few minutes later, the three of them stood.

"You're probably tired, Brian," McClane remarked. "It's getting late, anyway. Would you like to rest a bit and then join my wife and me at home for dinner?"

"That would be wonderful," Loeffler replied. "I eat in enough restaurants to make me appreciate home cooking more than ever."

McClane turned to Corey.

"Son, how would you like to break bread with us?"

The young man was clearly excited by that prospect. "Absolutely, Dr. McClane," he said. "I'd be honored."

Corey excused himself and headed back toward his dorm.

Corey returned to his room, which he shared with a student named Rob Walker. Outwardly they could hardly have been more dissimilar. Corey was intellectual, very thin, and despite the California sun, perennially pale. He was actually quite healthy, a young man decidedly not inclined toward athletics but very much at home with computers and scientific theories and the like. Rob was handsome, muscular, darkly tanned, and a world-class athlete, but actually on an intellectual par with Corey. The fact that they were brothers in Christ formed a bond that made them very close.

Corey noticed that Rob seemed quieter than usual, slumped in one of the two chairs in their small quarters, looking out the window, only grunting a mild "hello" as Corey entered.

Corey put his hand on the other's muscular shoulder. "Rob? What's wrong?"

"It's Laurie," Rob said. "She's disappeared, Corey."

Rob turned around. His eyes were filled with tears.

"I wanted to help her," he said. "I wanted to do something. God knows I did."

"What happened?" Corey asked, sitting down in a chair next to his friend.

"Her old man again," Rob said. "He beat up her mother, and Laurie conked him over the head with a paperweight."

"Did she kill him?"

"No! She's so small, you know, so tiny. I love her, Corey. I really love her!"

"Did she run away after that, thinking she'd killed her father?"

"Yes. She just split. Nobody knows where she is."

"And her father?"

"He regained consciousness in his wife's arms. Just as the ambulance was arriving, he attacked her. It was all the paramedics could do to pull him off."

"Rob?" Corey asked, alarmed. "Laurie's mother's okay, isn't she?"

"No, she isn't! She's dead. If Laurie ever finds out, she'll never come back."

Tears came to Corey's eyes.

"Rob, what can be done?" he asked.

"Only prayer," Rob replied. "We can only pray."

"Yes, of course, I'll start a prayer chain, but what about finding Laurie? The police—what will they be doing?"

"Everything they can, but you know they deal with thousands of runaways every year out here."

Rob paused, his hands visibly trembling, then said, "Corey?"

"Yes?"

"He killed her with a strange wood carving just like the one found here at the college."

6

McClane had invited someone else to join them at dinner: Dr. Roberta Maxwell, a robust clinical psychologist in her mid-forties who had formed, with county tax money, what she called the Hollywood District Commission on Ritual Assault.

"We wanted to say satanic assault," she said somewhat wistfully as they sat in the den of the McClane home after dinner.

"Why didn't you?" Loeffler asked.

Dr. Maxwell let out a flash of anger that fairly shook her formidable body.

"One individual," she replied. "That's all it takes, you know—just one."

Her eyes had widened, and there was a flush of red on her cheeks.

"I don't understand," Loeffler said.

"This person said that using Satan's name in that manner was a form of religious bigotry."

"What?" Loeffler responded, astonished.

Dr. Maxwell grimaced.

"Yes, I know. Truly absurd! But here—where we have a thriving hub of so much that is sustained by the most twisted logic—well, it's becoming rather commonplace, unfortunately."

She was thinking of the bizarre people with whom she came in contact on a daily basis, people who were chained to the worship of "holy" crystals, for example, who would do nothing without crystal in some form beside them or on their person, perhaps as earrings or a bracelet or a ring.

For many months, Loeffler had been hearing a growing crescendo of comments about Hollywood, a town never acclaimed as a pinnacle of old-fashioned values. The more recent developments made this city's previous immorality seem almost puritanical in comparison.

"We have the most awful suspicions about high officials in this area," Dr. Maxwell added, "including the mayor."

"As far up the ladder as that?" Loeffler asked, incredulous.

"Absolutely," she told him. "Marconi's been involved

in deals that have been successfully covered up until recently. What I am afraid of is that he will begin to act desperately, like the proverbial cornered rat."

"It sounds like there's a concentration of evil here," Loeffler said.

"It's true. When the man at the top is corrupt, you don't have to look far for corruption elsewhere."

"Why hasn't he done a better job of controlling the media?"

"Good question, pastor. Let's put it this way. All of us may loathe what the press does to slant the news, to manipulate it, to tell only the juicy tidbits. But that thirst for scandal can be a blessing in instances such as what we are now facing."

"You mean the press can't be bought off so easily?"

"Exactly!" she said, pleased at his perceptiveness. "But characters such as Marconi are only tips of a growing number of icebergs."

"That's so true," Charlotte McClane said suddenly.

Everyone turned toward her. She was in a chair to one side, next to the sofa on which her husband and Loeffler were seated.

A shy woman, rather like the stereotype of a town librarian, Judson McClane's second wife seemed a little embarrassed at the attention. But as she spoke, she seemed to tap some reservoir within her, and her face showed some very deep emotions.

"You can detect the growing changes," she continued. "So much of it is obvious. On the one hand, you have this awful increase in ritual-based violence, and yet the police seem more skeptical than ever."

She stood then, pacing.

"You have more action against prolife protesters than you do against those who are prochoice. Even our supposedly born-again assistant chief of police said, 'Despite my personal feelings, I must uphold the law.' "

She spun around and faced the others.

"They said precisely the same thing in Nazi Germany, you know."

"Are you saying that Satanists have infiltrated the police department out here?" Loeffler asked.

Mrs. McClane was trying to rein in her emotions.

"Tell him, Roberta," she said before leaving them and walking outside.

"Charlotte is coping with some new knowledge, knowledge so shocking that she hasn't been able to deal with all of it," Dr. Maxwell observed. "You see, my organization has uncovered the fact that, back in 1982, there was a secret national meeting of Satanists."

"Nothing like that has ever leaked out," Loeffler remarked. "At least not that I'm aware of."

"And we should ask ourselves why," Dr. Maxwell replied. "Could it have anything to do with those who are their allies in the media?"

Loeffler was stunned, even after having gone through the experiences at Providence Junction and what he had learned during months on the road.

"Here is what happened," she said. "We had an informant tell us, an informant who later died of so-called natural causes."

And clinical psychologist Roberta Maxwell began an astonishing story.

The year: 1982.
The location: somewhere in the Midwest.
The occasion: the Feast of the Beast.

Hundreds of Satanists had gathered at an out-of-the-way site, bringing tents with them so that they did not have to pay for motel rooms.

A speaker known only as Michael stood at a make-shift podium and addressed the crowd. "It is for an evil purpose that we gather here," he began as thundering applause greeted his remarks. "It is to hasten that time of dread that is foretold even in biblical prophecy."

His remarks were booed at that point.

Someone from the audience stood up and shook his fist at the speaker.

"How dare you mention holiness here!" the man shouted indignantly. "This is a time of evil. Do not spoil it!"

"It is biblical prophecy and the holiness of God from which it flows that we must array our forces against!" Michael shouted him down. "Holiness is our greatest enemy, and we cannot be victorious unless we understand that enemy."

The man grumbled a bit but sat down.

"Most of you remember little from those days when you may have been inclined to read Scripture. But that is one of the reasons I am here—to remind you of key passages,without the knowledge of which we truly will be sheep led to slaughter before the throne of God Himself!"

And he launched into a lengthy delineation of Scripture prophecy.

"You must realize that, according to God's plan, we are doomed from the start!"

He paused, letting that sink in.

"All of us one day will be thrown into the Lake of Fire to be tormented forever and ever."

A gasp arose from the multitude.

"That is what God *says!*"

This time there was a collective sarcastic chuckle.

"And millions of human beings have believed Him since our lord, Lucifer, was cast out of heaven."

The people stood and punched their fists into the air above their heads, shouting, "No! No! No! No!"

After they had gotten over that outburst, they sat down and continued listening to Michael.

"You say, 'No! No! No! No!' but it will *be* 'Yes! Yes! Yes! Yes!' unless we do better than we have in the past. We must spring forth more Hitlers, more Jim Joneses, more Gacys and others upon the world. We must rip and tear at the very fabric of civilization itself."

And he went on to outline a Satanist blueprint

through the year 2000, a striking manifesto, a detailed, meticulously organized plan for corruption followed by subjugation.

They knew that they had to proceed with vengeance. Sand was rapidly leaving the hourglass!

"There are certain areas upon which we must concentrate, beginning with the abortion clinics!"

"Babies will be very necessary—not the dead ones but those that survive. The live ones, ah, yes!"

He reached into his pocket and took out a hypodermic needle filled with a tiny amount of clear liquid.

"The foot soldiers of the future!" he declared. "Chained to us forever!"

He paused, relishing the moment.

"We raise them as our own," he continued. "There are no records to prove their existence. As far as the government is concerned, they're dead meat."

A collective chuckle arose from the crowd.

"We raise them, yes, and then we send them out into the world!"

He banged his fist down on the podium.

"But we cannot stop there," Michael continued. "There is an even bigger source for us."

"Day care centers," shouted someone from the crowd.

"*Exactly!*" Michael chortled.

But he wasn't finished, even then.

"The church," he added. "Corrupt the leaders and shake the flock to its knees.

"And the schools," someone shouted from the audience, "don't forget the schools."

"Amen," Michael said, "if you'll pardon the expression!"

Laughter. . . .

"Of course it didn't end there," Dr. Maxwell continued. "Their targets are the very foundations of our society, from churches to every level of government."

She went on to build a case for the coming corruption of government so extreme that it would make Watergate seem like a Sunday school lesson.

"You can hardly imagine the extent of attempts to get control of judges and senators and so many others," she added. "The judicial system is in bad shape but it will get worse."

Charlotte McClane had returned to the living room seconds before.

"May I, Roberta?" she asked.

Dr. Maxwell nodded.

"On top of all that," Mrs. McClane said, "you have Satanist groups releasing into society countless numbers of youngsters with destructive impulses that can explode at any given moment."

"Proverbial walking time bombs," Loeffler muttered.

"There is no better description," she agreed. "It explains someone taking an assault rifle and gunning down children in a school yard. It explains a mass murderer whose trial drags on forever."

"Whatever happened to our ethical standards?" Loeffler asked. "Where is public outrage these days?"

"Those who would have screamed the loudest then are now part of the problem," Dr. Maxwell pointed out.

"I suspect you are including churches in that."

"I am, unfortunately," Dr. Maxwell acknowledged. "Christians are supposed to be the salt that preserves this world of ours, but emotional excess seems to be replacing sound biblical teaching today."

"How well I know that," Loeffler admitted, thinking of his own failures.

"There's something else," Corey interjected, then told them about his roommate's girlfriend.

The minister's face turned ashen.

"Sir, are you all right?"

Loeffler recounted the role of the carvings when he lived in Providence Junction.

"What is their significance, sir?" Corey asked.

"They're a focal point for demonic forces, a kind of fetish."

"A key to unlock the occult?"

"Exactly."

"Poor Laurie," Corey whispered. "She's run away before."

"Let me guess," Loeffler said. "She also had gotten into prostitution. A huge percentage of runaways, boys as well as girls, end up on the streets as hustlers or hookers."

Mrs. McClane leaned forward.

"How much difficulty did Rob have when he learned about Laurie's activities?" she asked sympathetically.

"He got through the anger and shame and realized that he loved Laurie and couldn't desert her. He claimed her for Christ."

Dr. McClane turned to Loeffler.

"I have an idea. I wonder sometimes about the police doing their job, so Brian, why don't you, Corey, and Rob spend some time looking for Laurie yourself? I'll make sure they're cleared from their classes."

Corey's eyes lit up.

"The spots where the runaways work are pretty well known," he said. "Maybe the others will tell us stuff they wouldn't reveal to the police."

"Count me in," Loeffler agreed. "But what about the reason I originally came here?"

"That is important," Judson McClane said, "or I would never have stressed the urgency. But I suspect a day or two will not matter so greatly."

"Fine," Loeffler told him. "We'll start first thing to-morrow."

He stood, and so did the others.

"When do you want to leave?" the minister asked.

Corey looked at McClane.

"It's your call, son," the chancellor said.

"Tomorrow, sir?" Corey asked somewhat tentatively.

"No problem," Loeffler assured him. "Say, why don't you and Rob join me for breakfast? We can leave immediately afterward."

"I'll tell him," Corey replied. "It'll be fine, it'll be really fine!"

7

Henry Running Stream had not been able to forget Brian Loeffler.

My ancestry may go back to the time of the Aztecs who originated that little carving. We have lived centuries with our idols. Can you expect us to so easily sweep them aside?

As he looked at his son playing in the dirt and sand, he realized how little his own gods had come to mean to him over the past few years.

And River!

Gone.

With his wife dead and only little Lone Eagle left, he was feeling increasingly isolated from his own people, from the old ways, and especially from the old worship.

Ceremonies.

That seemed the bulk of what worship had been. A few rituals repeated over and over and—

My whole life has been filled with images of wood and stone and soil, and gods of wind and sun and moon and rain.

He had offered some fragile insight to Brian Loeffler, insight showing the tip of a very large and growing problem within himself.

It seemed that the gods no longer listened.

Yes, it was either that or—

Something else.

Something far more possible, he had to admit.

Something—

He shuddered at the thought of generations of worship crumbling around his feet, no more substantial than the dust and the sand.

And he realized quite suddenly that he wanted to talk to this Brian Loeffler again.

The next morning, in Loeffler's car, Corey turned to the minister, hesitation on his face. "Sir, there's one more thing you should know. Something Dr. McClane couldn't tell you."

"Go on," Loeffler encouraged.

"Something happened just before you arrived," Corey said. "There was a prayer meeting involving a dozen students. One of the girls started speaking in tongues. She went crazy."

"But there's nothing wrong with tongues," Loeffler protested, "only with the excesses to which a small portion of the movement goes. I slipped into that error in Providence Junction, too."

"Sir," Corey said, "she claims she was visualizing being with her dead mother, Dr. McClane's first wife. She claims she saw her mother approaching her. But not her mother as she was in life. It was her mother as though she'd stepped right out of the grave, after decay had set in."

"Why couldn't Dr. McClane tell me about this, Corey?"

"Because the girl was his daughter," Corey said. "Maybe it's still too fresh, too personal, but I thought you should know about it."

Oh, Judson, Loeffler thought, *my good, good friend!*

"Yes. Thank you for being honest, Corey. No wonder he was so insistent that I come as soon as possible!"

"Sir," Rob said after they entered the Beverly Hills city limits, "Laurie had a fascination for a particular spot. She took me there once and often talked about it. Could I show you?"

"Of course," Loeffler replied.

They had been driving down Benedict Canyon. Rob had him turn off, up a twisting, turning street named Cielo Drive, then on to a growth-shrouded driveway and stopped in front of a ranch-style house with a FOR SALE sign out front. The asphalt driveway was cracked and pockmarked, bulging in spots; the lawn was overgrown with crabgrass and other weeds; the house itself needed a fresh coat of paint.

Loeffler and the two young men walked up a slope toward the house.

"Nobody seems able to make a go of it here," commented Rob.

Little wonder, Loeffler thought, for he knew the history of this house, a well-known case. In the seventies, a hippie gang had murdered everyone in the house, seven victims in all. Five years later, the new owner committed suicide. A decade after that, someone had died of a drug overdose there.

Loeffler walked over to the edge of the property, taking in the view. It dropped off just beyond the chain-link fence on which he leaned lightly. Spread out below him were some of the more expensive properties in Beverly Hills, their value skyrocketing annually.

"So green and neat looking," he remarked out loud.

"Oh, yes," Rob said. "That's the point. The facade is orderly and well kept." He pointed to a house. "Over there is the home of the head of one of the studios," he said.

"I can tell by your tone of voice that you don't admire this guy."

"I don't. His films are terrible and his personal habits disgusting. But he's part of the power structure. Everybody's afraid of him."

Rob pointed to another house.

"The actress living there openly abuses her children."

"Openly?"

"Oh, yes. Nothing is done because she happens to be

a major box-office draw. They need her, so she does as she wants."

Rob hesitated a moment before indicating another house.

"You seem nervous," Loeffler observed.

"I am. That one would make any Bible-believing Christian nervous! She's the powerful columnist who's become a witch of the New Age movement. Her power is great in this town, too. She's into crystals."

"Back in Providence Junction it was pieces of wood carved by an Aztec knife used for demonic sacrifice."

"According to what I hear, quite a few of the homes that have crystals also have at least one of those carvings," Rob told him. "It's as though those little things are somehow links in a psychic chain."

Somehow a kind of link. . . .

Loeffler's mind went back to Providence Junction.

Countless thousands of misshapen creatures, some with gnarled faces and arms, taloned hands, eyes red with the rage they had felt for all of time, ever since being denied what they lusted for, the subjection of heaven and earth, even God Himself, Creator subservient to His creations, as they tried with awful dedication to displace Him from the throne.

And in their midst, their supreme ruler, one so unholy that Loeffler stumbled back, falling, but not before their eyes met, not before he felt hatred beyond comprehension.

" 'And Satan will probably use the debris of this transformed and debased house for the fuel to heat his hell,' " he said out loud, absentmindedly.

"What was that sir?" Corey asked.

"Remembering," he replied.

"From what I heard, those memories must continue to be quite awful," Corey said sympathetically.

"Is there a stronger word, son?"

"A stronger word?"

"Yes . . . stronger than awful?"

Rob threw his shoulders back.

"Laurie talked about tragedy so much," he said. "She had this feeling that nothing in her life was going to turn out right."

"I've worked with many abused children, Rob. You're shocked that Laurie would turn to prostitution, and that is a startling fact, but it's almost predictable in the case of girls abused by one or both parents. More than forty percent of the prostitutes in this country become prostitutes because of a desire to make all men pay for what was inflicted on them. They have an obsessive desire for revenge."

Rob turned away briefly to hide his tears.

As the three of them walked back down the tree-sheltered, winding driveway to the car parked on Cielo Drive, Loeffler turned and looked once more.

"There's still an odor," he commented.

"That's right. It must be our imagination, of course, but everyone experiences the same thing—the odor of old blood."

And scrawled in the red of it on one wall, an unspeakable blasphemy. . . .

Something caught Loeffler's attention: a multicolored reflection of the sun off someone's glass window or. . . .

He shrugged and got into the car.

Anita Carlsen put down the binoculars as she stood at the redwood railing of her back patio.

He's here. It continues, she thought.

She surveyed the homes below, smiling slightly as she realized that she had had contact with most of the residents—actors, actresses, directors, writers, others in the entertainment industry. *They listen because they are so hungry.*

Sighing, she went back into the house and made a phone call.

"I just saw him," she said into the receiver. "The reports were accurate."

She paused, listening, then: "But he will not find it so easy here. We've had years to do our job. Yes, tell the others."

She replaced the receiver in its cradle, her head tilted back, her eyes closed for a second or two. Perspiration dripped down the sides of her cheeks.

Finally she looked about her living room. It was quite modern in decor, the color scheme black and white: a black onyx fireplace set in a wide expanse of white wall; black carpets, white furniture, bookshelves built into one wall. Crystals were on the fireplace mantel, on the end tables on either side of the sofa, on almost every flat surface of the room. *Why do I feel so little harmony? That man can do nothing here. And yet there is such fear in my heart!*

She saw a Bible on one of the shelves and surprised herself by retrieving it, sitting down on the sofa, and leafing through it.

The Lord shall send the rod of Your strength out of Zion. Rule in the midst of Your enemies!

The Lord is at Your right hand; He shall execute kings in the day of His wrath.

He shall judge among the nations. He shall fill the places with dead bodies.

She rubbed her right arm, which suddenly felt numb, and read on.

And then the lawless one will be revealed, whom the Lord will consume with the breath of His mouth and destroy with the brightness of His coming.

She threw her head back, not wanting to continue any further but somehow compelled to do so.

And I saw the beast, the kings of the earth, and their armies, gathered together to make war against Him who sat on the horse and against His army.

Then the beast was captured, and with him the false prophet who worked signs in his presence.

She gasped, knowing how many she had led in the direction of seeking signs—not from the Bible but from crystals and the deep occultic powers these generated. She was a high priestess of the entire New Age movement, chosen because of her strong dedication and her dynamic presence. She could captivate almost any audience.

. . . by which those who received the mark of the beast and those who worshiped his image . . . cast into the Lake of Fire burning with brimstone.

No more! She could tolerate no more. And yet there was that final, awful passage, compelling and unavoidable: *And I will bring him to judgment with pestilence and bloodshed; I will rain down on him, on his troops, and on the many peoples who are with him, flooding rain, great hailstones, fire.*

She felt so very cold then, cold and strangely alone, a state of aloneness that was somehow more total than any she had experienced before.

And I will bring . . . to judgment . . . the many . . . who are with him. . . .

The shattering reality of such words hit her. *I am one of those*, she told herself. *I am one who faces pestilence and bloodshed.*

She closed the Bible and put it back on the shelf, hesitating there for a moment, tempted to take it out again and read more of its contents. *The master I serve coming to such an end?* she asked herself. *And with him I go . . . beyond the gates of hell.*

She left the living room, walked down a short hallway to a door at the end, and hesitated as she placed her hand on the knob. Beyond the door she could hear the familiar leathery fluttering of wings, could smell the cryptlike odor. As she entered the room, her manner was expectant.

"I'm ready, master," she said with a note of uncertainty she hoped would not be noticed.

Not a minute too soon, came the reply, slicing into her mind. *Not a minute too soon.*

8

Therefore God gave them up to uncleanness, in the lusts of their hearts, to dishonor their bodies among themselves, who exchanged the truth of God for the lie, and worshiped and served the creature rather than the Creator. . . . For this reason God gave them up to vile passions.

Romans 1:24–26

A few minutes later, they pulled in to the parking lot of a store that Loeffler never imagined he would be entering. As they got out of the car, Rob cautioned him, "You may not be prepared for this, sir. Laurie took her tricks here to get sexual things. I thought we could ask about her."

What he saw inside the store reminded him of what he had found just before Providence Junction went up in flames.

"It was different in Providence Junction," he said aloud.

"How's that, sir?"

"The occult and marital aids stuff was in a special section toward the *rear* of the local bookstore."

Corey nodded knowingly. "Yes, sir, it's more in the open than ever."

Loeffler felt an immediate sensation of oppression as he glanced over the objects displayed in the shop.

"We should leave now, my friends," he said, his discomfort growing.

Corey was standing next to him, but Rob had gone over to another counter and was asking about Laurie. He came back with a disappointed look.

"Nothing," he said. "Nothing at all."

As they walked toward the front door, they noticed a man in his mid-forties enter.

"I've never owned a thousand-dollar suit, but that sure looks like one," Loeffler whispered.

The bald man headed toward the rear of the store.

"He's a television producer."

"What's he doing here?" Loeffler asked naively.

"Getting supplies."

"And where does he go from here?"

"I'll show you."

A few minutes later, they were driving along Santa

Monica Boulevard, following the producer's car toward Highland Avenue. Loeffler saw a somewhat ordinary-looking section of Hollywood, with a supermarket, a couple of banks, a clothing store, a pawnshop, and bars.

"Look there," Rob said.

He pointed to a bar called The Gold Coast. Young men were entering as well as leaving.

"He'll go there to find a companion," Rob explained.

Loeffler noticed several teenagers standing on street corners, trying to thumb rides, and pointed this out to Rob and Corey.

"So many of them," he said.

"Sir, it's not rides they want."

"Oh." He felt so naive!

At least one of the boys seemed no more than fifteen, short, thin, uncertain as he looked at the cars that passed by.

"Where are the police?" Loeffler asked.

"They can't handle it all," Rob said. "They try, but they're spread too thin."

Through the rearview mirror, Loeffler could see the frail-looking boy being approached by a heavyset man. An argument seemed to be developing. The man grabbed the teenager.

Loeffler pulled over to the curb and got out of the car, walking quickly toward them. Corey and Rob were directly behind him.

The man was slapping the boy.

"Cut it out!" Loeffler screamed. "What in God's name are you doing?"

The man spun around.

"God?" he laughed, his voice guttural. "God's not the one in charge here!"

He pushed the boy to one side and started to lunge at Loeffler.

"I claim the protection of Jesus Christ and place myself beneath His shed blood!" the minister shouted.

The man stopped inches from him.

"You!" he exclaimed. "You're the one!" Then he turned and ran.

Loeffler ran after him, Rob following, while Corey remained with the teenager. The man ran down a street named Poinsettia and then turned left into a warehouse complex, entering one of the large structures.

Loeffler was only a short distance behind him. The door slammed shut behind the minister. He could hear Rob pounding on it, but his attention was taken up by what he saw in front of him: crystals, row after row of them. And hundreds of unopened boxes. But there were more than crystals— there were thousands of the little wood carvings!

The shelves containing the crystals and the carvings were to his left and his right. Directly in front of him was a large table with several open boxes.

He approached the table and saw five of the carvings packed into a box, ready for shipping.

"Familiar, aren't they?" the voice boomed out at him as though from loudspeakers.

Perspiration stuck his clothes to him.

In days gone by I would have cringed, he thought. *I would have tried to convince myself that it was all nonsense, that I was hearing things.*

No longer!

"Yes they are!" he shouted in reply. "They are the familiar dead relics of a condemned—"

Wings; the rustling of wings. He looked at the seemingly dead figures. They were moving, their wings fluttering.

Suddenly he heard a crashing sound.

"Another," the voice said. "Good!"

Loeffler looked to his left and saw Rob had found a way in. Just then, the creatures took flight, one after the other.

"Oh, God!" Rob said, stunned and uncomprehending. "Oh, God, help us!"

He turned and started to run.

"They're not real, Rob!" Loeffler called, stopping Rob in his tracks.

"But I see them!"

Loeffler tapped his forehead. "Up here!" he said. "It's all up here!"

Hundreds of the creatures dove for Rob. "I smell them! I feel them. I—"

Calvary's mount . . . the deepest— Rob remembered the words sung by a visiting gospel singer —*fed by Calvary's love, becomes a fire.* He found himself repeating them out loud.

"That's right, son," Loeffler called. "Train your mind on the Lord. They're not touching me because their master knows that I am on to him."

Rob fell to his knees.

"Dear Jesus," he said. "Dear Jesus, I claim—"

The creatures started disappearing into thin air, score after score.

Rob stood, looking at his hands and feeling his face.

"Not a mark!" he said, astonished.

"But what could they have been trying to protect?" Loeffler asked.

Rob, still shaken, had wandered over to some other boxes. He opened one and leafed through some documents inside.

"Sir, would you look at this?"

Loeffler looked at the sheaf of papers Rob handed to him.

"Notes of meetings," the minister mused. "I don't recognize the names."

"I don't know all of them, but there's one I do. Sir, he's an assistant to the mayor, specifically appointed as a liaison with the police."

Loeffler read from the notes: ". . . stopped the prosecution of Martin Andreno."

"Oh, the top Satanist in the nation," Rob said.

"But why would an assistant to the mayor get involved?"

Rob stood in front of him.

"It's a cesspool here, sir. You have no idea of the junk that's going on."

Loeffler took out several of the sheets and stuffed them into his pocket.

"Let's go," he said.

They went outside, back the way they had come.

Two squad cars had pulled up on the side street, and Corey and the frail teenager were talking to four police officers.

Loeffler and Rob hurried up to the group. Within a few moments after identifying himself, Loeffler had explained what had happened between the young boy and the older man.

"Do you know where the guy went?" one of the officers asked, apparently satisfied.

"No," Loeffler replied. "I suspect he fled through another exit."

He noticed that the teenager was handcuffed.

"Are you taking him into custody?" he asked.

"Yes, sir, we are," the second officer told him.

"But why? He's the one who was assaulted."

"The kid's a hustler. He's broken the law."

Loeffler could do nothing.

As he was climbing into the backseat of one of the squad cars, the teenager turned for a second and smiled wanly as he said, "I hope you find her."

And then both cars pulled away.

Corey looked at Rob.

"He's seen Laurie!" he told his friend.

"Where?" Rob asked.

"He gave me directions but said she might have moved on since then. Let's go!"

After getting back into Loeffler's car, they headed east along Santa Monica Boulevard.

"Hollywood isn't nearly as glamorous as it once might have been," Corey told the minister as they drove past a fast-food pizza parlor and noticed more teenagers trying to hitch rides. "When you make a left turn onto Highland, you'll see what I mean."

Loeffler knew what Corey was talking about as soon as he saw the sign: GAY AND LESBIAN COMMUNITY SERVICES CENTER.

"They're supported by five hundred thousand dollars in annual county funds," Corey added.

"Institutionalized corruption," Loeffler muttered.

"It is, sir. But doesn't the Bible forecast that sort of thing?" Corey pointed out.

Loeffler nodded, saying nothing just then, trying very hard to calm down.

They uncovered no other details about Laurie that day but were encouraged to know that she had been seen recently. At least there was hope that she was still alive.

The next few days, Loeffler spent more time on campus, learning the details of the situation that had drawn him to Four Gospels in the first place. McClane and several of the professors showed him various files dealing with matters such as discipline, test results, and other indications that McClane hadn't overreacted.

He talked to students who had been caught smoking marijuana as well as crack cocaine. One of them told a particularly revelatory story; his name was Rick Matson. The young man hadn't been expelled because McClane saw possibilities in him, a real chance for him to turn around.

Loeffler and Rick were sitting in the dorm room that Rick shared with another student.

"I got started when we all went into Hollywood one night," Rick told the minister. "Someone came up and offered me a marijuana cigarette laced with crack cocaine. He said it had a real kick to it."

"Why did you try it?" Loeffler asked.

"Curiosity. Simple curiosity."

"Just that, Rick?"

"Just that, sir."

The master of court intrigue and international espionage could get down to the level of enticing one young student through the mundane device of curiosity, of wanting to try something just once.

"Did you become hooked, Rick?" Loeffler asked.

"No, sir. I tried the stuff a couple more times, but I was caught here on campus before I was really into it."

"Crack cocaine is supposed to be highly addictive, isn't it?"

"That's the miracle, sir. The Lord intervened in time, in a very special way."

Loeffler heard other stories: one student was into pornography; another was gay. These problems and additional ones kept surfacing.

Back in McClane's office, Loeffler had posed a telling question: "Judson, how much of what you are seeing now has actually been around for some time?"

"I don't understand, Brian," McClane replied. "What are you getting at?"

"I mean, you've probably had gay students before. And students experimenting with drugs."

"Are you saying," McClane said somewhat angrily, "that perhaps I just didn't notice that sort of thing before?"

"It's possible, my friend. I can speak from personal experience!"

When Loeffler said that, McClane's temper quickly cooled.

"I've been down in the mud with the rest of them, as the expression goes," Loeffler added.

McClane sighed. "I admit that, at one point, I became so caught up in the success syndrome, in the image of a perfect Christian college, that I may have overlooked early signs."

He looked directly at Loeffler.

"I pray that it's not too late, Brian," he said sadly.

"With students like Corey and Rob and Rick—well, Judson, the Lord has plenty of worthy vessels."

"You think Rick is a worthy vessel?"

"Yes, I do. He's faced Satan directly and turned away. That's real victory."

After that first time in Hollywood with Corey and Rob, Loeffler went back to talk to street kids, waitresses, salespeople, even tellers at banks in the area.

The center of the so-called gay culture also held the main concentration of runaways. Turn the corner from the Gay and Lesbian Community Services Center, and there were two miles of one of the most infamous sections in the country, filled with gay bars, houses of bondage, and boys and young men making themselves available for perversion.

Loeffler talked with many of the young people, nearly all driven from their homes by abusive parents or otherwise intolerable conditions. Few pretended to like the life they were now leading. But he heard little about Rob's girlfriend, Laurie, until one day he, Corey, and Rob sat in a fast-food restaurant on Highland Avenue.

Loeffler's attention was caught by the sight of a robust-looking young man leaning against a parking meter and looking directly at him through the front window.

"See our friend there?" he asked Corey and Rob.

They looked outside.

"Yeah," Rob replied, "one of the Santa Monica Boulevard hustlers. Tough dude, that one."

Loeffler had to agree with that description. Roughly

twenty or so, the young man was wearing a dirt-smudged tank top and tight-fitting leather slacks. He obviously spent a great deal of time keeping his body in shape.

"Why is he waiting there?" Loeffler asked.

They found out as soon as they finished eating and left the restaurant.

The man walked up to Loeffler and introduced himself as Sam.

"Heard about you," he said. "Heard a lot about you."

"What have people been saying?" Loeffler asked.

"Not here," Sam said. "Can we take a ride?"

Loeffler nodded.

Corey and Rob got into the backseat of the minister's car, and Sam sat in the front.

"People have been saying you're looking for someone," Sam continued. "Is that right?"

"It is," Loeffler replied.

"Do you know where she is?" Rob asked.

"She's your girl?"

"Yeah, she is."

"Well, I know the last place she was before they took her."

"They took her?" Rob repeated words that seemed to hold all sorts of evil within them.

"Afraid so. She's no longer at this place," Sam said as he gave them the address, "but I thought you might find some clues there."

"Why are you volunteering this?" Loeffler asked. "Aren't you endangering yourself?"

"I live with danger, mister. It's nothing new. Besides, I'm tired, real tired."

"Tired of what?"

"The junk in my life. You see, they took a friend of mine, too. I couldn't stop them."

"You look big enough to stop anybody," Loeffler observed.

"Not when I'm stoned."

"How did it happen?"

"Like this. . . ."

Sam and his friend Ralph were on the way back to their apartment, walking along a street named La Brea, when a car pulled up at the curb to Sam's left.

"Get in," a rough-looking man growled at them after rolling down the window on the passenger's side. "In the back."

"Can't," Sam told him. "Not now. Come back later. We'll be around."

"Now!" the man said, louder this time.

The look on his face made Sam hesitate, though he was obviously bigger than this character.

"Let's go," he told Ralph. "We don't have to waste time with—"

Three men jumped out of the car, flashing knives at the two of them.

"Run!" Sam yelled.

Sam's strong legs carried him forward like a track star. Seconds later he heard Ralph scream, then headed back to La Brea and saw his friend being dragged into the car, his shirt soaked red.

"Ralph!" Sam had yelled as the car door slammed shut.

Ralph had an expression of utter terror on his face.

"I never saw him again," Sam told them. "I don't know what they've done with him."

Loeffler turned the car onto a side street and stopped for a moment at the curb.

"Sam," the minister started to say, "were you and Ralph—"

"Yes," he said softly before bursting into tears. Finally, wiping his eyes, Sam looked at Loeffler, Corey, and Rob. "I still try to convince myself that there's nothing wrong with it."

"But that doesn't work, does it?"

"That and nothing else. Not Ralph. Not the guys at any of the bars on Santa Monica Boulevard. They're all in the same pit, the same—"

"Hell? Is that it, Sam? It seems like hell, doesn't it?"

"Yes!" Sam said, nearly hysterical. "I thought, a few weeks ago, that I could finally do it, could finally stop all this garbage."

Suddenly Sam was drained of emotion, and his face became a cold mask.

"But that's impossible," he added. "I know that now. There isn't any hope, any change for my kind."

He opened the door and started to get out. Something slipped from his side pocket onto the front seat.

Despite himself, Loeffler flinched noticeably. So did Corey and Rob.

"You've seen this before, haven't you?" Sam said. "I thought I could do something with my life—until I got this!"

He grabbed the small wood carving and ran from the car.

9

As Henry Running Stream eased his battered and rusty Chevrolet onto the highway, he was not at all sure that he was doing the right thing. The emotions he found himself face-to-face with were not the ones to which he was accustomed.

He had long since given up any realistic hope of getting beyond a few dusty acres of doomed land.

At night, never with a truly filled stomach, Running Stream would listen to the sounds of cars on the highway, coyotes with their curious gibbering that was far more typical of the beasts than their only occasional howl, and sometimes the very slight hint of something hopping across the ground near the bed he and Lone Eagle shared.

At night he would often be awake and thinking that, when he died, he would leave his son the same miserable legacy that he had been handed by his father, Gordon Broken Bow.

It was all our land, he told himself, *the fertile areas, the forests where game was plentiful.*

The rage would almost choke him.

And now we don't even have the scraps!

Even so, he had tried very hard not to let hate overwhelm him. As he sensed victory in controlling this emotion, he would hear of something or go through an experience that would bring it to the surface again.

Lousy heathen, he remembered. *They called me a lousy heathen. I had to give up my devil gods or God would continue to punish me, to give me the fruits of my spiritual darkness.*

There were times he simply walked away. Other times, he fought. Through it all, he seldom found a white man he could trust. Until he met Brian Loeffler, who claimed to feel his pain.

And how many of you are shining examples of the god you claim to follow? You stole our land from us. You make promises, today, of a better life, and yet in truth you give us little or nothing. You hop into your shiny new cars and spit at our feet as you pass by.

And then there was this Loeffler, this Brian Loeffler.

I feel your pain.

The simplest of words and yet—

A stranger feeling some of his pain!

How could that be? Surely Brian Loeffler had spoken

113

words not to be taken seriously, words with as little meaning as "How are you?" or "You're looking good" or "How are the wife, the kids?"

And yet he yearned for it to be more. He yearned for the sincerity he craved, for the caring that his soul desperately needed. If he didn't get it, he feared where his emotions would take him.

Running Stream thought back to something a missionary had told him a long time ago, when he was still young. "Christ took our sins upon Himself," the kindly middle-aged man had told him. "Our pain became His so that none of us will ever have to suffer eternally if we simply accept Him. Henry, that's all it takes—simple acceptance, my dear brother."

Brian Loeffler was the second white man in Running Stream's life who seemed to care. He had said, "I can only hope that you, a decent man, see the truth."

What was this truth?

That was why he had left his son in the care of another family he could trust. That was why he decided to leave the reservation in order to track down the Reverend Brian Loeffler.

The building was only two blocks from Grauman's Chinese Theater, just off Hollywood Boulevard. Sam had sent them to an abandoned duplex that had never been occupied, the owner having run into financial problems before it was completed. The exterior was finished, but not the interior. Bare wood frames were visible in most of the rooms, exposed insulation in others.

Loeffler and Rob crawled in by lifting up a piece of planking on a hinge and squeezing themselves through a hole in the building's side. Corey thought it was a good idea to stay outside, in case they did find Laurie and she decided to run.

All the two of them found was garbage: ragged blankets, plastic cups, cigarette butts. Laurie wasn't there.

Rob picked up a single sheet of blue stationery crumbled up and thrown to one side, gasped, and then started to read:

> Dearest Rob:
> You may never get this. I don't even have money for a stamp to send it to you.
> I love you, Rob. God knows how much. But I'm too messed up. It's been going on for years with my father. I thought, at first, that what he was doing was "normal." Later, when I realized it wasn't, I doubted anyone would believe me. Anyway, he promised to hurt me if I blew the whistle on him.
> This time, though, I knew I had to get away, forever.

That was all.

Rob handed the sheet to Loeffler. *The sins of the parents*, the minister thought as he read it. After he had finished reading, he turned to Rob and said, "Lord willing, we'll find her, son."

"But in time?"

He had bent down and picked up something else.

A hypodermic needle.

"It may not be hers, Rob. You do realize that, don't you?" Loeffler pointed out.

Rob closed his eyes for a moment, his lips moving.

"I do, sir," he said finally. "I asked Jesus for strength and He just gave it to me."

Loeffler reached out and hugged Rob, and they walked back to where they had entered the building.

"So sad," Rob whispered.

They saw crumpled photos of families, pets, a wedding shot, a blond surfer posing beside his board; they saw a little square plastic packet with some flecks of white powder in the corners; they saw a Bible.

Loeffler picked it up and flipped through the pages. On one of these were scrawled just thirteen words: "Who am I? Where are You, God? Why can't I just be happy?"

He showed the page to Rob.

"Without Christ, everyone asks essentially the same questions, don't they?" Loeffler said.

"I know. I used to do that myself. I tried so hard to help Laurie find the answers."

As they were approaching the front, they heard confusion outside, and after emerging from the building, they saw a young man stumbling away from two cars that had just collided.

Corey rushed over to them. "He bolted right in front

of them," he shouted. "They tried to avoid him and hit each other!"

The young man ran their way. He stopped for a couple of seconds in front of them, then started to run again but collapsed only a few feet away.

Loeffler was the first to reach his side.

"Call for help. Quick!" he yelled.

The young man reached up and grabbed the collar of Loeffler's jacket. "Help me," he cried. "Please help me."

And in fragmented sentences he blurted out his story before the ambulance arrived.

It had been 9:30 P.M. The boy, Lane Connelly, had been walking with his girlfriend, Luci.

"Sir, can you help us?"

Lane had turned toward the voice as the dark blue van pulled up to the curb on his right.

A heavyset middle-aged man with a moustache smiled at him. "We're lost, son," he said pleasantly.

Lane let go of Luci's hand and walked up to the van. "Where do you want to go?" Lane asked, leaning through the open window.

"All the way, sucker," Lane heard someone say from the backseat, then he felt a piece of cloth pressed against his nose. He struggled, and as consciousness fled, he could feel himself being dragged inside the van. Just before he blacked out, he heard Luci scream and caught a glimpse of her rushing toward the van, managing to grab the driver's shirt. The driver shoved the palm of his hand against her nose, yet she still held on.

A shot rang out, and Luci was flung backward by the force of the blast. That was the last thing Lane was conscious of for some time.

When he finally regained consciousness, he felt sharp pain throughout his body and smelled the odor of damp hay. *A barn?*

He attempted to maneuver from his side to his back but could not. He was bound so tightly that he could move only his head.

My Jesus, I need Thee every hour.

He hummed those words to himself until he could stay awake no longer.

He had no idea what time it was when he came to again.

Voices.

And something else.

In the immediate background, he could hear munching sounds.

"To the lord of the Dark Pits," a man's voice exclaimed.

"To the Feast of the Beast," intoned another.

Lane was a seminary student. He knew satanic ritual when he heard it. *Dear Lord, help me,* he prayed. *Loosen these bound limbs.*

His hands were almost completely numb, but he found some play in the rope. He could not attract their attention. He had to be utterly silent. He felt pain as his hands hovered between feeling and virtual paralysis from the flow of blood being cut off.

One hand free! He reached back, carefully, trying to find the knot on the rope around his feet.

The men in the barn were consumed with their ritual; no one was looking his way.

Lane found the knot and pulled it loose. *Praise Jesus,* he said silently. *Praise Your Holy Name.* He changed position ever so slightly.

Suddenly there was some commotion outside the barn. The men jumped to their feet and rushed past the door, one of them shouting, "There's trouble! There's trouble!"

Lane worked quickly to free himself completely. He would have to risk the front door. There was no other way in or out of the barn. He peered around the edge of the doorway and saw the men near a house a few hundred feet to the right. He had to run for it; there was no alternative.

They spotted him even in the relative darkness, and two of the men ran after him.

Lane didn't see the ditch until it was too late. He tripped over the edge and fell into a mass grave. Controlling his nausea with a tremendous act of willpower, he climbed out and ran.

Seconds later, he was tackled from behind. They slapped him, punched him, kicked him. He had little strength to begin with, and even less now.

"Blessed Jesus, if it be Thy will, I am prepared now to

stand before Thy throne," Lane said as loudly as he could manage.

One of the men stumbled back.

The other yelled, "Just words, Josh. Just words."

"Jesus, Jesus, precious Jesus," Lane continued.

Josh pushed the second man aside. "There's somethin' different about him, Fritz," he screamed. "Different from the others."

As the two men struggled, Lane saw his chance and started running again.

"He's gettin' away, Josh! He can identify us."

"Let him go. I—I can't stand it anymore, man. I can't!"

Lane didn't stop until he blacked out again. The last thing he remembered was looking behind and finding that no one was following him.

The ambulance was heading toward Beverly Hills Medical Center, Loeffler in the rear with Lane, Corey and Rob following in a squad car.

"I tried to get help, but everyone shut me out. I must have looked awful to them . . . scared them . . . acted crazy."

"You're safe now, Lane," Loeffler assured him. "You'll be protected."

Lane tried to smile.

"Don't count on it, sir. I don't."

At the medical center, Loeffler, Corey, and Rob waited for a report on Lane Connelly.

"Did you believe what he said back there?" Corey asked. "I mean, it sounded a little farfetched."

"I believe it," Loeffler replied.

In low voices he and Rob told Corey what they had encountered in the warehouse.

They all stood as a doctor approached them, a grim look on his face.

"Your friend died minutes ago," the doctor said.

"What?" Loeffler blurted.

"Yes. Of internal injuries."

The doctor turned on his heel and started to walk away.

"Sir?" Loeffler said as he tapped the man on the shoulder.

When the doctor spun around, there were tears in his eyes. "I can't talk about it, pastor," he said, glancing around furtively. "I just can't," he repeated. "Not *ever!*"

"Why?" Loeffler asked. "Are you in danger? From whom?"

The doctor's expression was one of such fear that Loeffler cut himself off and let the man walk away down the corridor.

The three of them decided to head back toward the Four Gospels campus. At first they said little, unprepared as they were for the doctor's announcement and behavior.

. . . *your friend died minutes ago.*

How could that have been? He was in bad shape, yes, but to die so abruptly?

The doctor had acted quite scared. Could Lane, before he died, have told the man something so terrifying that he couldn't cope with it, couldn't answer any questions about it?

Loeffler kept his mind on driving, but he was also thinking about what had happened during the time he had spent in the Los Angeles area.

A familiar chill started at the base of his spine.

10

The underlying principle of all Satan's tactics is deception. He is a crafty and clever camouflager. . . . He does not build a church and call it the First Church of Satan—he is far too clever for that. He invades the theological seminary and . . . the pulpit. Many times he . . . invades the church under the cover of an orthodox vocabulary, emptying sacred terms of their biblical sense.

Billy Graham

Becky McClane could sense that something was going to happen.

She could see it in the way the attendants looked at her, the way the doctors talked to her.

She could sense something quite dark.

Quite terrifying.

It had happened in the midst of a tongues session in a new church she was attending. Strange words streamed from her lips.

I don't know what I'm saying, she remembered thinking at the time, an increasing feeling of panic overwhelming her. *I can't stop, I can't stop, I can't stop, I can't stop, I can't stop, I can't stop, I can't stop, I can't stop, I can't stop, I can't stop, I can't stop, I can't stop, I can't stop, I can't stop, I can't—*

Words without meaning.

Foreign. Harsh.

I want this to end. Please, please, why won't it end?

Finally it did end, when she fell into unconsciousness.

She was out for several hours. When she regained consciousness, everything seemed different to her. Her father and stepmother acted strangely around her.

"What's wrong?" she would ask.

"Nothing, dear. Nothing at all," they would reply hurriedly, unconvincingly.

She knew they were lying. Something had happened to her. They knew what, but they didn't want to tell her. *What's wrong with me?*

Money.

That was what the pastor promised. Money from heaven.

God, the best banker in the world!

But what about the Bible, sir?

It's like a passbook, Becky.

The Bible?

Oh, yes. Wonderful financial advice, dear. Listen to God and you can be rich.

But the Bible says that it is harder for the rich to enter heaven than for a camel to go through the eye of a needle.

Only a figure of speech, Becky. Don't pay much heed to that.

What is real, then, sir? What parts do we accept, and what do we ignore?

Let your heart tell you. Let your emotions decide.

My emotions?

They'll be your guide.

And not the Bible?

So she let her emotions out in a massive surge that night.

And in a language she could not understand, *something* spoke, *something* she let enter her very being through her ignorance.

I come, Becky McClane. I come, and there is no room for any other.

An image in her mind drove her to the edge of a psychological and emotional precipice.

Not of a person.

Not of any kind of grotesque animal.

A place.

Barren. Cold. A place of utter desolation, where a howling wind was the only sound.

Where God did not enter.

And another pushed her over.

A room.

No chairs.

Only a single coffin at one end.

She walked up to it, looked into it, saw—

A rotting corpse.

She stumbled back.

A *squishing* sound.

The body rose, climbed out of the coffin, stood there, staring at her.

She couldn't move, despite the grotesqueness of the figure only a few feet away, the odors of death, disease.

That mouth opened.

Words came from it, a voice distorted yet oddly familiar.

We'll never be separated again, Becky. I promise you that!

The figure started toward her.

It was only inches from her.

A hand reached out to touch her.

She fell into a dark abyss, screaming.

And she continued screaming, in reality, not in that awful nightmare. She screamed so loud, so long that blood gushed from her mouth and over the white-smocked figure in front of her.

Later, they told her she had evoked Satan, had called up the powers of darkness from black pits of foulness.

She beckoned, and they responded.

It wasn't her regular church. She had been trying

others, tired of her family's evangelical correctness, tired of turning to the Bible for everything, tired of restrictions.

And she found one that seemed just right.

So happy, she remembered. *So warm! So Friendly!*

She soaked in joy that seemed to hang in the very air around her. People touched people. People laughed, cried, sang.

It was so seductive, so total, so much a contrast to what she had known that she failed to see one ingredient was missing: any clear-cut indication that the Bible was at the center of their worship, even a verse now and then. There were plenty of copies in evidence but seldom opened, seldom—

And then that tongues service.

And then—

Anita Carlsen's hand was sweaty as she held the phone receiver next to her ear.

"Yes, I know we have him where we want him," she said. "But—"

She paused, listening to the man's voice at the other end.

"I am nervous because he has some degree of national prominence," she continued. "There is bound to be attention in the media, even if he is never found. There will be questions. Will we have all the right answers?"

She grimaced as the other person raised his voice.

"Okay," she said, "I will be the bait."

She hung up the receiver, going over the details in her mind.

Reverend Brian Loeffler was to be led into a trap, and she would be the bait dangled before him.

Over the past few months, what with his travels across the country, he had become a rallying symbol for antioccult forces in the country. Wherever he went, there was media coverage, and none of it was favorable to the New Age. He had the ability to be devastatingly on target in his observations.

So much on target, she thought, *that one of his arrows hit me.*

She had been watching a newscast involving Loeffler. At one point he admitted how weak he once was and how that weakness helped bring about the holocaust at Providence Junction.

"And yet I had no idea that this was the case," he had said. "My pride convinced me that I was on the right spiritual track."

Four of those words lodged inside her mind, and she could not brush them aside: *My pride convinced me.* And she knew he was also talking about her. Pride was a cornerstone in the foundation of her life, if not the entire foundation itself.

I'm in demand everywhere as a speaker. My agent has commitments for me that stretch on for two years. People believe what I write in my column, what I say in my books and speeches. O God, she said within herself, but not profanely. *O God, they are pointing their fingers at me, the woman who midwifed their doom!*

Mayor Adrian Marconi had summoned Anita to go over the plan. She was clearly nervous when she arrived at his City Hall office and sat in a chair in front of his large rosewood desk.

He was a short man, bald, with narrow eyes that seemed permanently shut. He had been mayor for several terms. The people liked him, and he used that public support with gusto.

"I'm transforming this city," he told her proudly. "I've got supporters in every department, in the media, in the gay community, everywhere. In time this will be a New Age mecca, Anita."

Anita summoned up enough courage to come very close to bursting the mayor's bubble.

"There's power here that we've not faced before," she ventured.

"That's nonsense, Anita. Loeffler's only a man."

"He's different."

"How can that be, Anita? In any event, we're going to be rid of him very shortly."

"I don't know, but I feel things, Adrian."

"Of course you do. You're psychically sensitive. We all know that."

"But there's more, Adrian. Only a few survived Providence Junction, and he was one."

"That's rather obvious, Anita. What's the point of all this?"

"He's alive for a reason."

Marconi snorted contemptuously.

"You aren't going to give me a speech about God's will, are you?"

She hesitated, knowing what she wanted to say but realizing the danger.

"He survived despite everything that Satan could throw against him. Do you have any idea why?"

"Not the foggiest."

"The point is that I don't either. We have to be very careful where this man is concerned."

"All of them will be dealt with as they start to be impediments to our progress. You know that. Please, Anita, relax!"

"I cannot."

Marconi stood.

"We're wasting time. Another ceremony tomorrow night! I'm looking forward to it."

She glanced at him, and he could tell that she wasn't looking forward to the ceremony at all.

"Good-bye, Anita," he said, wearing an altogether false smile.

When she had left the office, he leaned back in his chair.

"Dangerous," he said out loud. "She's going to do something to hurt us. I can smell it in the air."

He felt some unaccustomed emotion, a fleeting shred

of gratitude for all that Anita Carlsen had done to help over the years.

"If only you could have stayed the course," he whispered with genuine regret.

He reached for the phone on his desk, hesitating but a second.

"Those plans of ours?" he said after a brief wait. "Include Anita Carlsen. She's not indispensable."

He slammed down the receiver and leaned back in his chair, wondering for a moment why his left cheek was twitching.

Anita stood in the spot so many called Shangri La, just off the Pacific Coast Highway on Sunset Boulevard.

Surrounded by palm trees, blessed with an atmosphere of isolation from the frenetic world just outside its boundaries, it was superficially a place of meditation for all religions.

How gullible they are, she thought as she stood before the lake in the center of Shangri La. *They believe whatever we tell them.*

But there was no joy this time, she had to admit. She had a curious feeling of oppression.

That's a switch! she told herself ironically. *Usually others react that way.*

Not this time.

As she tried to meditate, tried to channel her mind in the right direction, the truth poked on through and she couldn't bury it, no matter how much chanting she did, chanting that had worked so well before.

The babies.

That was what got to her eventually.

The babies. Chained to the occultic group by the drug habits forced upon them.

She brought her hand to her mouth, suddenly feeling quite sick.

That night, sleep didn't come easily to Anita Carlsen. She got out of bed and walked into the living room. It was all there—her incense, her meditation pillows, the other implements. But this time she had no desire to use them.

After years of being a proponent of the New Age, Anita was having deep-seated second thoughts. Everything had been fine as long as it involved crystals and chants and pop pseudopsychology. It was fun for a while. But something had changed over the months: something deep and dark had crept in.

She picked up a newsmagazine and turned to a specific page: an interview with Brian Loeffler after "The Demonization of Providence Junction," as the article referred to the events in that town.

At first she was tempted to dispose of it without reading more than a few lines. But she stayed with the interview, reading every word.

"The New Age movement is a wolf in sheep's clothing. It seems so soft and cuddly and warm. One day, not many years hence, it will turn into the lion of Satan, devouring those who have been gullible enough to fall under its spell."

Shivering, she momentarily put down the magazine. "It seemed so soft and cuddly and warm," she repeated out loud.

That was indeed what attracted her to the New Age promises—rebirth without a great deal of anxiety; pleasure-filled days and nights; and no pain as a price to pay.

Everyone she knew felt similarly.

"It was all so *pleasant*," she spoke softly to the emptiness of her house, "with no risk. It was what we all had been aching for."

She hugged herself, remembering what it had been like earlier and thinking about the course of her life at present. Now there was only suffocating perversity!

As she reached for the telephone next to the sofa, she realized how violently she was shaking.

11

Judson McClane listened to what Loeffler and the two students told him. After they had finished, he leaned back in his chair, glanced at the plaques on his wall, the awards he had been granted over the years, the personal photographs in front of him on the desk.

"I want to tell you about what happened to my daughter," he said. "You know only part of the story, as do most of the students here. But it seems clear to me that each of us is now part of some kind of inner circle. Perhaps the Lord has something special in mind for us. Who can say? But I think you should hear the rest of what happened to Becky."

McClane closed his eyes and recalled events that he would carry with him for the rest of his life.

"Becky was never the same after that tongues session. Right now she is in a sanitarium. Something happened in her mind, something that was intensely corruptive." He sighed as he opened his eyes. "I don't blame what is clearly a gift that God has continued to bestow for two thousand years."

"Then what is at fault, Judson?" Loeffler asked, knowing the answer but wanting Corey and Rob to hear it as well.

"The human propensity toward excess," McClane replied. He reached into a drawer of his desk and brought out a pile of pamphlets. "Look at these," he said, holding up one. *"How to Become God Through Faith."* McClane grunted as he read those words. "Becky got that one through sending a donation to a television preacher."

Anger started to well up inside Loeffler. He had had his run-ins with that charlatan.

McClane raised a hand to make his next point.

"I hasten to add that there is nothing wrong with the electronic church itself, except that Satan has crept in and seduced many of its biggest stars. And are these guys ever experts at deception. They have that godly veneer, but underneath is the same old reconstituted gnosticism or some other old-line heresy.

"Think of the influence such blasphemy has upon young minds. This individual told hundreds of thousands, if not millions, of listeners that faith in Christ enables each of us to become God."

McClane showed them another pamphlet. *"Riches*

Guaranteed for Every Believer. God is portrayed as a heavenly chancellor of the exchequer, deliriously dispensing huge sums of money out of His delight that yet another unsaved person has become a born-again believer!"

"And Becky became hooked?" Loeffler interjected.

"Mind, body, and soul. But these are only the tip of the proverbial iceberg. Here's another: *Christianizing the Occult*. This was obtained from another television ministry. The contention is that Satan counterfeits so much of what God does and the counterfeit is quite evil, so we can turn the tables on Satan and counterfeit what he does. In this way we convert evil to good."

"Now that's a new wrinkle!" Corey exclaimed.

"Indeed it is," McClane agreed. "What it led to in my daughter's case, was a Christian séance. She thought that a séance done properly could establish contact with her mother."

"She actually went through with it?" Loeffler asked.

"Completely. And she's never been the same since. She has to stay locked up, probably for the rest of her life. At least that's what I thought until hearing what you and Rob encountered."

"I don't understand," Loeffler admitted.

McClane swung his chair around and faced the wall, his back to the three, obviously trying to get his emotions in check. When he faced them again, his cheeks were moist.

"I was so much like you once were, Brian," he continued. "I stood in the midst of this campus and praised

God for its beauty, praised Him for its healthy bank accounts, gave praise for the material blessings, while the spiritual aspect of life here took a backseat.

"I saw young people apparently quite happy, untroubled by drugs, carrying Bibles around with them, attending classes taught by Christian professors. I saw a dream that had become reality, and I thought us all safe!"

He stood and walked over to the large window in his office.

"I put my faith in the rewards, not the Giver of those rewards. I worshiped the blessings, not the One who blessed us. Oh, I didn't completely ignore Him, of course; He was out there somewhere, a kind of good-luck charm, I guess."

He turned from the window.

"Brian, would you visit my daughter? Would you see if you could somehow reach her?"

Loeffler didn't hesitate to tell his friend that he would go the next morning. Corey and Rob left, but he stayed behind at a gesture from McClane.

"Is there something else?" he asked.

"Yes, Brian, there is," McClane said. "I received a call from Anita Carlsen not long before you arrived."

"The New Age columnist? What in the world did she want?"

"She said that something is going on."

"Was that it?" Loeffler said, a note of sarcasm in his voice.

"She said that within the next few months, this city will become governed completely by practicing Satanists, that there would be other cities across the country succumbing, and that the biblical prophecies would be increasingly manifested as reality."

"What caused her to suddenly confide in you?"

"Babies."

"Babies? You don't mean—"

"I do. But not only them. The older ones. The runaways."

Loeffler had to stand.

"And this place has become the runaway capital, hasn't it?"

"It has. Thousands of kids a year. Walking the streets. Fodder for whoever gets hold of them."

"For whatever purpose."

Laurie, Rob's girlfriend!

"You're not alone in thinking that," McClane said.

Loeffler realized he must have been thinking out loud.

"And the young man you mentioned," McClane added. "Can you be sure he really is dead?"

Lane Connelly!

"I wonder about my daughter, Brian," he said. "Is she somehow involved?"

Loeffler sat down again, emotionally depleted.

"It's going to be worse than what went on in Providence Junction," he mused dejectedly.

"We are, after all, a major metropolitan center, with a

population a thousand percent greater than a small town like Providence Junction."

"With much more control of the media."

"Much more."

McClane pulled out a copy of the Bible from a bookcase behind him.

"These are the times of the fulfillment of prophecy, Brian," he said. "You know that as well as anyone."

McClane seemed reluctant to tell him something.

"What is it, my friend?" Loeffler prodded gently.

"This woman wants to see you, Brian. She wants to talk with you."

Loeffler found that curious but interesting.

"Did she say why?" he asked.

"She claims that you are in grave danger."

"Do you believe her?"

McClane frowned a bit.

"Anything is possible out here, Brian. I'd be inclined to suggest that you see Anita Carlsen."

"Where does she want us to meet?"

"She wants to meet you at the sanitarium where my daughter is confined."

Loeffler rested in his quarters, thinking of verses McClane had quoted.

And God gave them over to a reprobate mind. . . .

He had read it so many times over the years, but increasingly the significance grew as he saw events that would have been unthinkable a year or so before the tragedy at Providence Junction.

And yet what happened there is being eclipsed, he told himself.

And then there was Becky McClane.

Confined for an indefinite period of time because she had had an occultic experience so traumatic that—

What was her connection with a celebrated proponent of the New Age?

Becky McClane was awakened by the sound of someone singing. The voice seemed strangely familiar.

"Is there nothing but grief in this world? Nothing but pain? Nothing . . . nothing . . . nothing, oh, man, but despair."

The words came through, but there was no rhythm in the voice, no sense of melody.

Several minutes passed, and the voice disappeared, replaced by the normal silence of the institution, the sound of someone sobbing, a bit of laughter, an occasional scream.

Becky walked to the door of her room. In the upper third was a single window, small, square, of unbreakable glass. She could not see very far down the corridor, but it seemed empty. She started to turn away, then out of the corner of her eye she saw movement. It was a man, walking as though very weak, stopping every yard or so and leaning against the wall for support. He was coming directly toward her room! Finally he stood looking at her face framed in the window.

"Becky," he started to say, "somebody's got to be told what's—"

He looked older than he actually was, his skin so pale, his eyes red-rimmed and bloodshot, his frame so thin.

"They're coming!"

In an instant he was being wrestled to the ground by two very tough-looking men. A third, in a white smock, jabbed a hypodermic needle into his left arm.

"Too late . . ." he mumbled as he quickly lost consciousness.

Becky turned from the door and leaned against it, tears streaming down her cheeks.

"River," she said weakly before sliding to the floor, unable to stay on her feet any longer.

Henry Running Stream was lost. Instead of ending up on Pacific Coast Highway and heading toward Four Gospels Christian College, he had gotten onto the wrong freeway and found himself in a run-down section of Los Angeles.

Directly ahead he saw a rescue mission with people lined up outside, waiting for food and beds to sleep on. He pulled up to the curb across the street from the two-story building and sat there for a few minutes, looking at those in the line. Finally he got out and approached a man who seemed to be in charge, introducing himself.

"My name is Rex Blackburn," the other replied. "I'm director of this mission. What can I do for you?"

"I don't know. I got lost."

"Where were you headed?"

"Four Gospels Christian College."

"Fine institution. Fine indeed."

"Do you know how I can get there?"

"I do, yes. But won't you come inside and have lunch with us?"

"But I am a stranger, sir. Why would you want to share your food?"

"We all are strangers to one another, but not to the Lord," he said.

Henry Running Stream was hungry and everything tasted especially good.

Why am I staying here so long? he asked himself. He had no answer except that Reverend Blackburn, like Brian Loeffler, seemed more sincere than other white men he had met over the years. He could sense in them a real desire to help anyone who needed it, without passing judgment on them.

A short while later, as they were sitting in Blackburn's office, Running Stream asked him about demonic influence among those cared for by his staff and himself.

"What makes you interested in such matters?" Blackburn asked.

Running Stream hesitated, not only wanting to find the right words but also trying to organize his thoughts.

"I see the world. I hear things. I consider what my son River Brooks was flirting with before he left home."

"The occult?"

"Yes, the occult."

"I understand what you're saying," Blackburn replied. "More and more, I, too, see evidence of such activity. But then anything that drives a man to destroy himself has to be satanic at its very root, even if weird apparitions don't show up to announce the fact."

"Does that include bitterness?" Running Stream asked.

"Absolutely. You have had plenty of experience with bitterness, haven't you?"

"I have, sir. I have."

Running Stream stayed for several more hours, learning more about the functions of Reverend Blackburn's ministry.

Finally, Running Stream cleared his throat and asked, "Sir, have you ever seen one of these?" He took a small wood carving out of his pocket.

The color drained from Blackburn's face. He abruptly stood and asked Running Stream to follow him. They stopped in front of a door marked STORAGE. Blackburn unlocked it, and they walked inside. The minister pulled down a cardboard box from a top shelf. It was quite heavy, and when he lost his grip on it, the box fell to the floor, tumbling out its contents: dozens of the carvings.

Running Stream bent down and compared them with the one he held.

"Identical!" he exclaimed.

Abruptly the door, which had been left ajar, slammed shut behind them.

"What in the world?" Blackburn said as he tried the knob. "It's locked!"

He spun around as he heard Running Stream yell. The carving he had been holding was no longer inanimate wood. It was moving!

Running Stream dropped it.

"Look!" he said. "The others!"

They were squirming. One by one they seemed to be coming to life, stirring, the wood now a kind of leathery flesh.

"To your knees!" Blackburn commanded.

"But I am not a Christian," Running Stream protested.

"Do it!"

Running Stream relented and did as the minister had pleaded.

"Lord Jesus, I—" Blackburn started to say, then stopped when the light in the storage room went out.

Running Stream let out a yell.

Standing in front of them, surrounded by the tiny figures now alive, was something else: a shape—tall, thin—draped in black. Its outline was faint in the darkness. There was a hood over its head, and from beneath it flashed flame-red eyes.

Why do you stop your prayer?

The voice came from inside them, it seemed, piercing their minds, not their ears.

The figure reached out to Blackburn, its hand a grotesque split talon like the pincers of some hideous lobster. The talon closed around the minister's neck.

Running Stream lurched at the figure. It turned toward him, the hood slipping from its head, and Running Stream froze, unable to move.

It was sheer evil. The face was cankered around those awful red eyes, the lips were thin and also red, the teeth jagged.

You don't know who I am, do you?

Running Stream could not move or reply.

I am all the false gods before whom you have ever bowed. The figure lifted Blackburn off the floor. *And my power is now transcendent. My power—*

"Pray," Blackburn managed to say.

"But I—"

"For God's sake, pray in the name of Jesus!"

Running Stream started to speak words he barely remembered from his childhood. "The blood of Jesus!" he cried. "The blood of Jesus was shed so that—"

"—our sins could be forgiven and—" Blackburn's voice was filled with pain.

Running Stream bowed his head. "Satan's evil *can* be

stopped. We claim the protection of Jesus Christ . . . through the power of the Holy Spirit!"

The room abruptly shook several times.

Running Stream opened his eyes.

Blackburn was lying on the floor; the cloaked figure had disappeared; the light was back on; all the wood carvings were as they had been before, except one.

It stood before Running Stream, looking straight into his eyes. The animated figure raised a deformed hand and pointed at him.

The most intense chill he had ever known radiated through every inch of his body, and he fell to the floor, gripping himself, shivering.

Then the figure tipped over on its side and was transformed, before their eyes, back to wood.

Blackburn crawled over to the other man.

"Your neck!" Running Stream exclaimed. "There's not a mark on it."

"Because nothing here was real. I should have realized that right away, but he caught us off guard."

No one else in the mission was aware of what had happened. Even so, they could see that both Blackburn and Running Stream were pale and shaken. Two of the minister's assistants helped them to the mission's infirmary.

"Shut the door," Blackburn said kindly, "and lock it for a moment."

One of the men did just that, and the minister told them what had happened.

"I can only conclude that Satan now has us as a special target," he said finally.

"Maybe it was only me," Running Stream suggested.

"Or both!" Blackburn said with funereal emphasis.

Running Stream left a short while later, after deciding to head on toward Four Gospels and Brian Loeffler. Somehow he knew Loeffler needed his help—and that for the first time in his life, he felt this way about a white man.

Five blocks away he stopped, tears streaming down his cheeks. "I don't know the words," he whispered, "but I know I need help, too. I cannot go into battle unprepared."

He turned the car around and headed back toward the mission, knowing Blackburn would help him find the words he needed. He had seen the truth in Brian Loeffler and Rex Blackburn, and he wanted to be part of that truth himself.

12

Anita Carlsen had stopped just down the road from the sanitarium that overlooked Mulholland Highway between the San Fernando Valley and Sunset Boulevard, on a few level acres of ground surrounded by the Hollywood Hills. She picked up a portfolio from the front seat and looked through the contents, her hands trembling slightly.

Here's everything, she told herself, *everything I've heard and done over the past five years.*

Loeffler saw the woman waiting in a car near the entrance.

As he got out of his car and walked toward hers, he had the same sort of feeling he'd experienced back at the house where the multiple murders had occurred, that of being watched.

The woman must have seen him in her rearview mirror. She got out of her car and met him.

"I'm Anita Carlsen," she said.

"Brian Loeffler," he replied.

They shook hands.

"I wanted you to meet me here because of a certain young woman."

"Becky McClane?"

"Yes."

"What connection do you have with the girl's condition?"

"Reverend Loeffler, she was an experiment."

"An experiment?"

"Yes. We wanted to see if one of us could attend a tongues-speaking session and steer it in the wrong direction. If we could do that, then we could plant a member in these meetings all over the country."

"Corrupt the entire movement from within!"

"That was the plan."

"Where people often don't understand what is being said but depend solely on their emotions, they are fair game for devious counterfeits," Loeffler mused.

"That was what we were banking on, in every tongues-speaking congregation throughout the country."

"That's actually part of the plan?" Loeffler asked, disbelieving.

"Oh, it is, it is," she told him. "We are planting supporters in such congregations in community after community, state after state. They fit in very well. Once they are in positions of real influence, they will shift the emphasis entirely away from a biblical base to an emotional one."

"So their value for the cause of Christ is completely nullified! But did you intend such an extreme reaction from Becky?"

"No. We wanted to corrupt her, not destroy her. We hoped she would be a considerable asset."

"So why are we here?"

"I want the two of us to be alone with her. I want to ask her to forgive me. If she won't listen to me, perhaps she will to a minister."

Once inside, they approached the heavyset woman at the front desk.

"Hello, Anita," she said. "It's been awhile. What are you here for?"

"To see Becky McClane," Anita answered, her voice trembling slightly.

The woman's eyes widened a bit.

"Gone," she said. "Transferred."

"What?"

"Just this morning."

"I wasn't informed."

"Look, Anita, I know nothing about it."

"Who ordered the transfer?"

"Mayor Marconi."

Anita looked sharply at the woman and turned away toward the entrance, Loeffler following her.

As they were going outside toward their cars, the heavyset woman reached quickly for a buzzer under her desk and pressed it three times as she smiled cynically.

"Where could they have taken her?" Loeffler asked as they stood outside.

"I suspect I know," she told him.

"You know?"

"I can't be sure, but they have a camp off the Pacific Coast Highway."

"Near the Bible college?"

"A few miles away, deep within the Santa Monica Mountains."

Three very big men came running out of the sanitarium.

"Marconi's bullies," Anita said.

"Your car's closest!" Loeffler replied.

She nodded, and they dashed for the car as the men ran toward them. The ignition sputtered once, twice, a third time.

Marconi's men reached into their pockets and pulled out pistols with silencers on them.

Finally, the engine turned over; Anita spun the wheel around and headed away from the men.

Suddenly, seemingly from nowhere, a fourth man

jumped onto the road a couple hundred feet ahead of them.

At least he started out looking like a man, but in an instant he was changing into something altogether different!

"Don't pay attention!" Loeffler yelled. "It's a trick. I've seen it before. Go!"

She pressed down on the accelerator. The car made contact. The body was thrown over the hood and against the windshield, cracking the glass but not shattering it, and the body tumbled onto the road.

"It *was* human!" Anita exclaimed.

Loeffler quickly took off his jacket and wrapped it around his arm to push away the glass hanging somewhat tentatively in its metal frame.

"I've seen that—that thing—before. It's been in my house. I've . . ." She glanced quickly at Loeffler. ". . . bowed before it in worship."

The route they took went along Benedict Canyon, near Anita's residence. She checked her rearview mirror. Nothing.

"I want to stop here," she said, "to give you an idea of the way I've been living."

"Can we afford the time?" Loeffler asked.

"I don't care. I *have* to show you!"

As they proceeded toward the house, Loeffler noticed that the area looked familiar.

"Is this near where that gang slaughtered—" he

started to say as he noticed a Cielo Drive street sign.

"It is," she admitted. "I can look from my front porch right into that property."

"Were you doing that one afternoon when I was there with a couple of college students?"

"I was."

"And you saw us?"

"I did."

"I think I knew that."

"Oh?"

"I saw a reflection, like off some glass. It seemed a little eerie, for some reason."

"My binoculars," she said. "It must have been sunlight off my binoculars."

They arrived at her house in less than five minutes.

"Something's wrong," she said as they got out of the car.

"How do you know?"

"I feel it."

There were no other cars around, but as soon as they approached the front door and opened it, Brian realized how justified Anita's apprehension was.

It looked as though a wrecking crew had plundered the interior. Furniture was overturned; artwork had been flung from the walls; statues were lying in pieces on the parquet floor.

"It's all ruined!" she yelled. "I spent years collecting all this!"

She walked through the debris in the living room to a hallway and down the hallway to a closed door at the end, Loeffler following her.

"There is where *it* was," she told him. "It controlled me. I left my self-respect out here when I went into that room."

"But you seem to have broken away," Loeffler said. "How did you manage that, Anita?"

"I prayed for help, and I got it," she confessed.

Loeffler realized that Anita was hanging on to sanity by a slim thread, so he started to turn her away from the door and back down the hallway.

"No, Brian," she said, her face twitching. "You've got to see what's behind that door."

"But that thing."

"It's not here."

"How do you know?"

"Look!"

She pointed to the bare wood floor. It had been severely damaged. Whole chunks of the wood were torn up, and long, wide scratches marred the full length of the hallway.

"They look like claw marks," Loeffler said.

"They *are* claw marks. It's been taken elsewhere. I'm no longer the guardian."

"Then let's go."

"There's more to it than that."

She pulled away from him, grabbed the doorknob, and started to open it.

Instantly it was yanked out of her hand, and the door was flung open.

There was no room as such facing them. The wall directly opposite them had been replaced by a scene of such intensity, such horror, that both of them pulled back immediately.

"It looks like something out of Dante," Loeffler said, barely able to speak.

"Oh, it is exactly that," Anita replied. "This, Brian, *is* hell!"

It was an awful cavern, with corridors leading from it all around its circumference, and, in the center, looking like the inside of a volcano, molten rock turning shades of red and orange and yellow. Frightful creatures took human beings and threw them into the blazing inferno. There could not have been much of a difference in terms of the torment experienced because the cavern itself erupted geysers of flame through cracks in the floor, the rough-hewn walls, and even out of the ceiling.

"O God! Save us! We are ready now for Your salvation!"

Loeffler's eyes widened. "I know some of them!" he said.

"So do I," Anita added. "My mother is there. My father, Brian! My sisters, my brother. I see them all."

There were teenagers from Providence Junction; the mayor; members of his old board of deacons. Scores of people, all trapped, all being ravaged by the monstrous demonic entities that were there by the thousands, a shrieking, deafening horde of them.

"Shut the door, Anita!" Loeffler yelled.

She seemed transfixed by the scene, unable to break away. She actually started to walk into the room. "I deserve nothing better than this," she said. "This has to be my destiny."

"It is *not!*" Loeffler said, grabbing her by the shoulder and pulling her back, then slamming the door shut.

She started to fall, and he caught her.

"It's an illusion, Anita," he told her. "Hell is real, and the view of it we saw just now was probably correct, but *that* wasn't the doorway to hell. There's no such thing for any of us until our physical bodies actually die."

She looked at him with some relief before she passed out.

Anita regained consciousness in a few minutes.

"I want to go inside the room," Loeffler said, "to check it out."

"I'll go with you," Anita told him.

"You don't have to."

"I must, Brian, without any fear. I can't let fear dominate me any longer."

The two of them had been sitting on a sofa in the living room. Loeffler had gotten some towels from a nearby bathroom, moistened them with cold water, and returned to put one towel across her forehead while he used the other to wipe down her cheeks and neck.

Finally, they stood and entered the hallway again.

"Every night I would go inside and find it waiting for me," she said.

"Couldn't you stop?"

"I thought so. But later, I realized what was idle speculation and hope on my part and what was hard, evil reality."

"And that was when you started praying."

"Just after you arrived in town, Brian."

They were at the door. Loeffler opened it, and they both walked inside.

The odor was nearly overpowering—a mixture of decaying substances and overflowing cesspool—but the scene from hell was no longer there, now that they knew it had been in their minds, not reality.

"Look!" Anita said, pointing to the floor.

Loeffler bent down, touching the pool of liquid.

"Green slime," he said, disgusted. "The creature doesn't even have blood in its veins!"

"Does that mean it was hurt somehow?"

"I don't know."

Anita turned just a few inches.

"Over there," she said, "in the corner."

It was a pile of white feathers.

"What could they mean?" she asked.

"A great deal," he replied.

"But what?"

"Let's just say that the Lord has been known to intervene in miraculous ways."

Otherwise the room was utterly empty. They left, each sighing in relief, and Loeffler slammed the door behind him.

13

Anita insisted on driving, but Loeffler questioned her ability to do so safely.

"But *you* can drive, right?" she asked.

"Well, yes."

"Because you're a man, and men are stronger than women, whose emotions bruise more easily. Is that what you're saying?"

Loeffler smiled. "Okay, Anita, you win."

For a while it seemed that they weren't being followed as they headed up the Pacific Coast Highway toward Four Gospels.

"Strange, isn't it?" Anita remarked.

"Very," Loeffler agreed.

He looked behind them and saw a white car pull off

on a side road while a red car sped onto the highway from the same direction.

"I think I know their game," Loeffler told her. "Let's see if it happens again."

A couple of miles ahead, the red car pulled off the highway and a gray sedan replaced it.

"That's it!" he said. "We've been followed, but not by one car."

"We're dealing with some clever people," Anita pointed out.

"Tell me more," he said. "Why did you get involved?"

"My career was sagging, for one thing. I'd run out of things to write about. Then I heard about a new production company called New Age Productions. It sounded like good material for a column or two. An appointment was made with the president, Giovanni Marconi."

"A relative of the mayor?"

"His brother."

"Very cozy."

"Indeed. Anyway, he had some crystals in his office, and he told me that the name of his company had been carefully chosen. His people had done a marketing survey and found that the name New Age was a good one because the movement itself was going to become increasingly popular."

"But it was more than just clever marketing, wasn't it, Anita?"

"Much more. I got into the movement itself, hook, line, and sinker. When my next book became a bestseller, my career started to revive. I felt really good then."

"What started your disenchantment?"

"I found out that the crystals and the chants and the charming cocktail parties and that sort of thing were only surface elements. Something much darker remained underneath. I was invited to attend a ceremony. I managed to control myself at the time, but on the way home, I had to pull over to the side of the road. Brian, I can't begin to tell you what went on there. It was so *vile* it's almost beyond imagining!"

"Were there other things that changed your mind?"

"Oh, yes!" She was fighting to keep herself under control. "I learned some of their plans for this area and elsewhere around the country. By the year 2000, they will try to have everyone who hasn't become a Satanist living in moment-by-moment fear of their lives. It will be awful! What is happening now is but a hint."

"Through a glass darkly," Loeffler suggested.

She was weeping while trying to drive.

"Families will be torn apart, child abuse pitting parents against their children, and eventually the children will rise up and fight back. There will be fathers shooting their little babies, teenagers knifing their parents, the elderly being gunned down in mushrooming numbers. Governments will stink with corruption. Churches will become infested with heresy!"

Suddenly Anita screamed. Cars blocked the road ahead, just three miles from Four Gospels.

Anita instinctively swerved off onto a side road.

"Where are we going?" Loeffler asked.

"I have no idea!" she replied.

The road twisted and turned erratically, first on an upgrade and then down. To their right was a drop of hundreds of feet or more to a rocky bottom. On another occasion the Santa Monica Mountains would have provided some fine sight-seeing, but this time the drive was nothing short of dangerous.

Police sirens wailed behind them.

Anita didn't anticipate the sharp turn directly ahead. She tried to compensate but was too late. She swerved to the edge of the precipice to their right, half the car hanging over the abyss, the back half still on the road. The strong odor of gasoline was unmistakable. It was obvious that any sudden movement could send the car over the cliff.

"How can we just stay here?" Anita asked, not much short of hysteria. "They're just behind us."

Seconds later, a state police car pulled up. Two troopers got out and walked over to them. "Reckless driving!" the shorter one said loudly.

"Probably on drugs," the other added.

"I bet if we opened the trunk, we'd find all sorts of evidence."

"Agreed! Now what *should* we do?"

They started laughing as they turned back to their own car.

A minute passed.

"What are they waiting for?" Anita asked.

"Satan's emissaries are very good at tormenting people."

"Brian, *you've* got to survive. I've done too much damage already. I don't matter."

"We both have to—" Loeffler protested.

"No! Listen! On my left, a few feet down, is a ledge. Does it extend over to your side?"

Loeffler saw that it did.

"Try to make it, Brian."

He started to protest.

"I won't be going to hell, Brian. Don't worry about that. I accepted Christ into my life yesterday."

He was astonished.

"Thank God, Anita!"

Still the troopers hadn't moved. Loeffler wondered what was keeping them, and then he saw the answer. He could sense its presence more than see it, a vague feeling of something nearby.

"That sound!" Anita exclaimed. "I've heard it before, in my house and at that awful ceremony."

"So have I," Loeffler replied. "Back in Providence Junction."

The sound of leathery old wings rustling to life.

In an instant it had materialized directly in front of them, hovering just beyond the hood of the car, reptilian in countenance, with a body of green scales in stark contrast to its dark, leathery wings.

The thing reached out one taloned hand toward the hood and pressed downward, rocking the car forward. Then it stopped, repeating this action again and again, something resembling a smile crossing its demonic face.

"We're going over, Brian!" Anita said in terror. "We're—"

"No, we're not!" Loeffler declared. "Take my hand. Pray with me!"

She joined him in a prayer for protection through the shed blood of Jesus Christ. They both could feel a sensation of turbulence, as though a tornado were about to swallow them up.

The creature pulled its talon back instantly.

"In faith believing," the two of them said, "we beseech Thee, Lord, return this demon to the very pits of hell."

The creature's wings started beating at an accelerated rate. It looked upward suddenly.

"Wings again, Brian!" Anita cried. "But not the same . . . not the same!"

Just as back in Providence Junction Loeffler had witnessed a parting of the veil between the demonic world and the natural one, this time he saw a parting of the veil between the earthly and the heavenly.

Angels! Hundreds, perhaps thousands of them, a stream of iridescent beings visible for only a rare moment, overwhelming in their beauty. At first there were none, and then suddenly they appeared, surrounding the creature. They were cloaked in a radiance almost blinding in its intensity.

The creature lashed out at them, first to the left, then to the right, in an obviously futile attempt at defending itself. Abruptly it burst into flame, its screams tearing the air.

But it was not yet defeated. It would take two human beings with it, but not Anita Carlsen and Brian Loeffler. Instead, groaning with intensified agony, it turned from their car to the troopers directly behind it.

The two men tried to back away but could not move quickly enough. The creature seemed to melt then, becoming a wave of molten substance, glowing red like flowing lava, and pouring over the two men.

Their car ignited, exploding into a thousand glass and metal fragments.

The shock waves hit Anita Carlsen and Brian Loeffler instantly, causing a groaning sound of protesting metal.

"I don't want to die, Brian!"

The car shook once, twice! Metal was being torn loose from the undercarriage.

"Go, Brian! You are the one who—"

The car started to slide over—slowly at first, then faster.

"Jump, Anita!" he begged. "Please jump!"

"I can't, Brian. My door's stuck. Go!" she screamed. "In God's name, go!"

He swung open the door on his side and jumped out.

Loeffler caught a glimpse of his new friend in Christ bowing her head in prayer as the car slipped rapidly down the side of the mountain before exploding in flames as it hit the rocks below. Blackness engulfed him, but just before sudden wrenching contact with stone and dirt, he saw an image he would never forget: a smiling Anita Carlsen, her face lit with iridescent brightness, stepping through the gates of heaven, the sound of trumpets in transcendent harmony accompanying her.

14

Pain in his back.

In the midst of darkness, movement produced jolts of pain that made Loeffler pause, not wanting to risk any that might be worse.

He opened his eyes slowly, light coming in wavering patches, then steadier, broader bands of it, and finally—

The ledge.

He was still there.

It was rather wide, this natural outcropping of rock, and he could not easily tumble off it, but it was also quite hard, littered with smaller fragments of rock and stone that played their part in producing the pain that had wrenched him back to consciousness.

Odors.

Like that of charcoal.

Burning.

And crackling sounds.

He turned his head, saw just beyond the edge a cloud of smoke coming from below, black and—

Anita!

He moved suddenly and paid for it with pain, then looked over the ledge.

The flames had died down to thin little spurts from the wreckage itself. The nearby straggly clusters of brush were burned to a crisp, but thankfully there was no raging fire.

Loeffler managed to get to his feet and look around him. He could climb up to the road or down to the base of the canyon and make his way, quite blindly, in one direction or the other. It would be a shorter, safer climb up, but this choice was taken away as a car appeared on the road and stopped just above him, so he climbed down from the ledge and hid directly under it, on a much smaller ledge that was partially earth, very dry, and not at all firm. He flattened himself against the rock when he heard voices, praying his footing would hold.

"It's a pity we lost two men," someone was saying. "But at least those two are out of our hair."

"But mayor, look what happened to our men!" another said.

"Don't be paranoid, senator," the mayor replied.

"Just put it all in the hands of our master. He knows best; you can be sure of that."

Loeffler heard an approaching siren, car doors slamming, footsteps on the road above him.

"Tow it away now!"

"Yes, sir! What about the wreck down below?"

"That, too! I want no traces of any of this."

"The bodies?"

"Cremate them. Dispose of the ashes."

Loeffler eased his way down to the base of the canyon, one cautious footstep after another, while the men above dealt with the wrecked car on the road. He knew he had to get away, but where would he go?

The little camp was hidden in a section of the mountains not near any of the primary canyon roads. It had become, over the years, a favorite place for lovers, drug dealers, criminals, others. At one point the Manson family had spent time there.

Loeffler was nearly exhausted by the time he came upon the camp. He had picked his steps carefully in getting down from the secondary level, trying hard not to make any noise and succeeding in that goal.

Once on the valley floor, he found himself in the midst of unfamiliar territory. On both sides of him were mountains. He walked down a parched and dusty creek bed. Every so often a lizard skittered across his path. He was conscious of the fact that he was in rattlesnake country, but that seemed the least of his worries.

And then he saw the altar.

Bones were piled on it, scattered among gray ashes. And at the base a rusty knife.

He smelled something carried along on a cool breeze past his nose.

Meat cooking.

Cautiously he walked past the altar. Less than half a mile ahead, the creek bed curved to his left, and he followed it until he came to a natural cul-de-sac carved out of the mountain by the elements over countless centuries.

Ahead he saw three individuals—two young men and a woman—sitting around a campfire. The scene seemed peaceful enough, and he decided to show himself. He was obviously more unkempt than they were, and no apparent threat, so the three merely grunted after looking up and surveying his appearance.

"I need help," he said as he approached their little group.

"Mister, the whole world needs help," the taller of the two young men said cynically.

"Yes, it does. I'm a minister, and I know exactly what you mean."

The young woman smiled as she glanced at him a second time. "Your kind's been saying we're headed for hell for a long time. That it?" she said knowingly.

Loeffler nodded. "That's true."

"But no one listened, and now it's too late," she continued.

"Never too late, miss," he said somewhat lamely.

"Hope in the Lord?" The second young man finally spoke. "Is that it?"

"Exactly," Loeffler assured him.

The young man stood and threw his head back as he closed his eyes and let out a single yell. The sound returned as an echo that quickly died out.

"That's all there is," he said, turning back and facing Loeffler. "We make a little noise, and then it's over until someone else comes along and gets his chance."

His two companions grunted their agreement.

Loeffler felt a surge of pity for the three young people in front of him.

The woman stood suddenly and extended her hand. "I'm Rebecca," she said. "No reason for us to be unfriendly. All we have in life is one another."

Following her lead, the other two stood.

"I'm Marty," the taller one said.

"And I'm Karl," the other added.

"Brian," Loeffler responded. "Brian Loeffler."

They sat down around the campfire together.

There was an awkward silence until Marty cleared his throat and spoke up. "Brian, you look like you've had a bad time of it. What's going on?"

Loeffler told them a little of what had happened. As he talked, he realized that he was beginning to like the trio, even though they were pretty wild looking. Marty and Karl had very long, stringy hair, well-worn jeans, spotty complexions. Rebecca had a tough look, a streetwise manner that looked wrong on someone that young. Even so, there was a fragility about their manner that clashed with the cynical exterior all three projected.

Searching. . . .

They claimed to have found the real answer to life, which was, in their view, that there were no answers to anything, and they were doomed to drifting purposelessly perhaps for the rest of their lives.

And yet—

The search hadn't ended, despite what they claimed. They still clung to some kind of hope, some bedraggled thread of purpose, yet they had no sense of what that purpose was.

Marty shivered as he rubbed his beard nervously.

"That means the whole city is being taken over," he said. "And if a senator is involved, then—"

"The state government, too," Karl added.

"Do you know a large college around here?" Loeffler asked.

Rebecca nodded. "Three miles west of here," she said. "Nice campus. You been there, pastor?"

"I have," Loeffler told her. "Have you?"

The three of them laughed.

"They don't want our kind there!" she exclaimed.

"Pastor, you came from the east," Marty said. "Have you noticed anything strange?"

"Other than what I told you?"

"Yeah."

"Not a thing. What do you mean?"

"I have a friend," Marty continued. "She disappeared."

"When?" Loeffler asked.

"A few days ago. That's why we're here."

"What makes you think she's in this area?"

Marty was about to answer when his chest exploded in an outburst of blood as a rifle went off a short distance away.

The others spun around to see a figure duck out of sight around the corner of the cul-de-sac.

Marty was on the ground, crying. "God help me," he begged. "God help me."

Loeffler went to his knees beside Marty.

"Pastor, I don't want to die without—without Jesus," the young man said as his body started to twitch uncontrollably.

"You won't, son, if you—"

"Jesus, I accept You as my—" Marty said, coughing away the rest of the words. He smiled at Loeffler, and mumbled, "I've heard the words before, pastor." He reached his left hand upward in a gesture of supplication, then the hand fell back against the hard earth.

Rebecca started weeping.

"I'm going after that . . ." Karl screamed as he turned and raced toward the opening of the cul-de-sac.

"No!" Loeffler called after him.

This time there was the sound of several rifles. Inexplicably, Karl was still standing.

"Run!" he shouted. "Into the cave! Hurry!" Only then did he fall to the ground.

Loeffler and the young woman headed toward the opposite end of the cul-de-sac. He saw the cave almost immediately. They were just at the entrance when Rebecca fell into his arms. He dragged her into the cave and saw that she had been hit in the shoulder.

"Please go. Leave me, pastor," she begged as they rested on the cave floor.

"I won't," he said. "How can I?"

"Because of this," she said. "I can hold them off while you get a head start and —"

She pulled a pistol from the army jacket she was wearing, seconds before the first figure appeared at the mouth of the cave.

She swung the weapon up, in an apparently instinctive move, and fired it, hitting the man in the temple.

"His rifle!" she said. "Grab it!"

The weapon had fallen forward a foot or two into the cave.

Loeffler hesitated, then dashed to the rifle and picked it up. He caught a glimpse of half a dozen armed men advancing toward the cave.

"We didn't explore much of this cave," Rebecca said as she leaned on his shoulder and the two of them hurried forward, "but there are so many twists and turns that we can probably shake those guys."

They hopped or stumbled or walked ahead for quite some time. During one brief rest period, Loeffler examined her wound and saw that the bullet had just grazed the flesh.

"I'll be fine," she said. "I've been through worse than this."

The cave system was a natural maze, with tunnels shooting off from one another to such an extent that Loeffler doubted he could ever find his way back outside.

Ahead was a wall with figures etched into the rock. Loeffler started to examine them, then pulled back.

"What is it?" Rebecca asked.

"Like Pompeii," he told her.

"Obscene?"

"And satanic."

The further on they went, the more rock etchings they found.

"I can see what you mean," Rebecca said, looking at one. "That's pretty gross."

Both were tired. After walking a bit farther, they sat down for a few minutes.

Rebecca was not at all like many of the street people Loeffler had met over the years in rescue missions across the country or church-sponsored halfway houses. She had the same hard edge, yes, but there was something else.

"I gave up on God," she said, "because I thought He'd given up on me."

"What about Marty and Karl?"

"They never believed in much of anything but I liked them," she said, trembling. "In their own way they were honest, good people."

"But it's not *anyone's* way that decides—only God's."

"Can you imagine the kind of life they—I—have had for the past few years?"

"I can."

"So much dirt, pastor. So much. . . ."

They stood and started walking again, Loeffler trying to reassure Rebecca that God's forgiveness wasn't subject to withdrawal.

The tunnel they were in curved to the right. As they turned the corner, they entered another, a higher one that was also considerably wider. At one end it opened in a huge cavern. And in the middle, grouped in a circle directly ahead of them, were six crosses stuck upright into the ground.

Henry Running Stream saw the patrol cars ahead, blocking the highway, and pulled off on a side road, hoping that no one had spotted him. He slung a quiver of arrows over his shoulder, grabbed a bow, which he had crafted himself, and left the car there, going on foot.

Bow and arrows, he chuckled to himself as he realized how he was armed. *The authorities still don't make it easy for Indians to get any kind of gun. How little anything changes.*

The area was mountainous, the highway cutting through outcroppings on one side. Running Stream was well accustomed to such terrain and managed to get to within hearing distance in minutes, catching bits and pieces of conversation.

"Dirty business," one of the officers said.

"Yes. I don't like it one bit. The mayor's a real nut case."

"I wish we had never gotten into this stuff."

"Same here."

Suddenly they heard an explosion not very far away.

"Look!"

"What the—"

Running Stream saw it immediately—a cloud of smoke nearby.

"Should we?"

"No. We wait here until someone says otherwise."

"I agree. We don't stick our necks out any more than we have to. We stay right here."

Running Stream moved on. By the time he made it to the site of the explosion, two men had just hopped into a nearby car and were driving off.

He waited several minutes, then came out from behind a large boulder, slid down onto the narrow road, and approached the twisted wreckage.

There were two bodies just outside it, blackened beyond recognition. But something else was on the floor, something familiar.

He backed away. *Just like my son's,* he thought.

A siren. For a moment he hesitated, then ran back across the road and away from that place.

15

Loeffler walked up to the crosses, reached out, and felt the wood.

Rebecca approached. "Lots of holes," she said, pointing to the cross beam.

He looked up.

She was correct.

Nail holes. Dozens of them.

"At the base, too," she added. "What could have gone on here?"

"Rites," Loeffler said.

"Rites? With crosses?"

"Yes. One of Satan's great joys is counterfeiting and perverting many aspects of God's plan for mankind."

"People were *crucified* here?"

She made a face and turned away from the crosses. Suddenly she whispered, "I hear voices."

At first he thought it was her imagination, then he heard the voices himself.

"What are they saying?" she asked him.

He could understand nothing; no language was being spoken that he had ever heard before. More frightening than that was the accompanying orchestration of chilling sounds: hissing, as from modern-day dragons . . . growls, guttural, threatening . . . sounds like vagrant gusts of wind through a drafty house, mournful, rattling doors, creaking floorboards.

And the leathery sound of wings fluttering!

"I don't *see* anything," Rebecca gasped. "But I hear—"

"Satan plays tricks," Loeffler told her. "He likes to play on the mind and the emotions."

And play Satan did with the two of them. Awful faces popped out of the darkness at them.

"We've got to leave," Rebecca begged.

"Delusion," Loeffler said. "Simple delusion."

A taloned hand in front of her face!

She screamed. "It scratched me!" she said in panic. She turned her face toward him, and he saw a cut, with blood seeping out over the edges.

"How could that be?" he puzzled.

The Bible was quite clear about the reality of demons. Could it be true that they were *never* visible, that *everything* Satan threw out in his bursts of oppression was strictly fantasy, strictly manipulated imagination? Or could some instances be real?

Then they heard words echoing off the walls of the cavern, obscenities flung at them with great rapidity, followed by utter silence.

Loeffler and Rebecca looked at each other, then around at the cavern, its ceiling a hundred feet above them.

Rebecca moved her left foot slightly and nearly slipped on something wet. She bent down and, touching the surface, held up her fingers.

"Blood!" she exclaimed. "It's blood."

"A recent ceremony," Loeffler surmised.

"I don't have anything to wipe it off with," she said.

"Here. I have a handkerchief."

Loeffler was reaching into his pocket when a loud and very cold voice filled the cavern.

"No need to bother. There will be more."

Half a dozen figures stood in the entrance, all but the middle one holding rifles.

"The mayor!" Rebecca told Loeffler. "It's the mayor of Hollywood."

The middle figure reacted with laughter.

"How nice it is to be famous," he said, stepping forward. "I am Adrian Marconi. And you must be the famous Reverend Brian Loeffler. Since when have you started hanging around with whores!"

Rebecca reacted instinctively. "I have been a whore, yes," she said, walking toward the mayor. "But any pimp I ever had was Sir Gallahad compared with swamp scum like you!"

The smile disappeared from Marconi's face. "Shoot her!" he ordered.

Rebecca turned toward Loeffler. "Maybe I'll greet you at the gates," she said as the shots rang out, then her body jerked spasmodically and she hit the ground like a very limp doll.

Marconi walked up to Loeffler.

"She won't be missed," he snarled. "But Anita Carlsen—that's another story. Because of you, she is dead! She was one of our most valuable—"

"Puppets!" Loeffler spat out the word. "Automatons conditioned to do the bidding of your infernal master. Anita finally saw the truth and severed her links with demonic lackeys like yourself."

"Call it what you like. She helped us!"

"All those things she said?" he blurted out.

"She was telling the truth," Marconi assured him. "How much had you suspected before now?"

"Some of it."

"But the rest startled even you?"

"Yes."

"Providence Junction didn't mark the beginning, you know," Marconi continued. "But it was a watershed. It showed what massive power could do."

"And how many lives could be destroyed in a very short period of time."

"Yes. That must have been the fun part."

Loeffler lunged for the mayor, but two men easily pulled him away, holding him tightly between them.

Marconi seemed amused. "How easily you resort to violence," he said, smirking.

"Christ did the same thing when He threw the money changers out of the temple."

"Oh, yes, Jesus Christ. The model for all Christians."

Marconi reached into a shirt pocket and took out a small sheet of paper. As soon as he had unrolled it, he showed the drawing on one side to Loeffler.

"*Our* model!" Marconi proclaimed proudly.

"How can you serve such a master?" Loeffler asked with disgust.

"How can we turn away from him?" the mayor replied, a slight suggestion of regret in his voice.

"Are you saying he has made you powerless?"

Marconi nodded. "Sometime ago, we might have . . ." he started to say, then, after shrugging his shoulders, he added, "Who knows?"

His expression hardened again. "But it's different now," he said, "very different."

"What are you going to do with me?" Loeffler asked.

"Show you what you've been seeking."

Loeffler was grabbed roughly and taken from the cavern, then driven a short distance in a van. What he saw when the van stopped was unexpected; the surroundings were somehow familiar.

Marconi approached him. "You act as though you've seen this place before," he said knowingly.

Loeffler nodded.

"It's been the set for more than one television series," Marconi explained. "They used to be just facades. Now they've been turned into actual buildings, with their make-believe fronts remaining."

Just then a little girl wandered out of one of the buildings and came up to them, holding out a flower toward Loeffler.

"She's welcoming you," Marconi said. "Take the flower, please."

Loeffler reached out toward her. "Thank you," he said.

And then she sank her teeth into his hand.

At a command from Marconi, the little girl pulled back.

Loeffler's hand was throbbing.

"Not all that seems innocent is," Marconi said.

Loeffler was feeling quite weak.

The mayor ordered one of the men in the van to get a doctor.

"We'll be in his room," he added.

Loeffler was helped up the street and into a western-style building that doubled as a hotel. Once they reached the room that had been set aside for the minister, someone arrived to treat the wound.

"I'm Dr. Barnett," the short, middle-aged man identified himself. "I suspect it feels worse than it is."

"But why would she do that?" Loeffler asked.

Barnett looked at Marconi.

"Because she's been thoroughly trained," Marconi replied, "as have the others."

"The others? You have more like her?"

"Many more," Marconi said boastfully.

"But why?"

"They must depend upon us for everything and be exactly what we want them to be, now and later."

Marconi paused, lost in thought for a moment.

"Later they will be released into society, boys and girls grown up and ready to take their place in the world around them."

"But they'll be psychological freaks, time bombs ready to explode!"

"That is the purpose of all of this!" Marconi said, a note of triumph in his voice.

Barnett's face twisted into a grimace.

"I'll leave you in the good doctor's hands," the mayor said to Loeffler. "One of my men will be stationed down the hallway if either of you need help."

When they were alone, Loeffler seized the opportunity to talk to Barnett.

"You don't like what they're doing here, do you?"

Barnett, who had nearly finished dressing the wound, avoided his gaze.

"No, I don't," he said simply.

"They why do you cooperate?"

Barnett unbuttoned the left sleeve of his shirt and rolled it up to the elbow.

"My habit is very exotic and expensive. They are my only source."

Loeffler saw an arm pockmarked with holes; some of the veins had been so abused that they had collapsed, causing ugly indentations.

"I suppose this sort of thing shocks a minister," Barnett said. "I can understand why. But it is standard practice in this cult and in others around the country. They like to get women who are drug addicts and pregnant and indoctrinate both mother and child."

Barnett was becoming nervous.

"You'll heal nicely. I can't stay any longer."

He turned toward the door.

"I wish I could do more," he said, his words slightly muffled. "I never stop wishing that."

"And yet you *do* nothing."

Barnett didn't answer as he shut the door behind him.

Loeffler was confined to the room for several hours. No one approached him. He could only doze fitfully on the bed or stand at the window and look outside.

He saw a great deal of activity. Police squad cars pulled up, officers got out, stayed for a while, and then left. He saw a limousine stop just in front of the hotel, a dapper-looking man in his late thirties get out, and the car pull away. The rear license tag read U.S. SENATE.

He stepped back from the window, stunned. A senator at a camp run by Satanists! Where did the chain stop? How much beyond the senatorial level did the Satanist influence ascend?

*   *   *

Asleep, Loeffler realized that it was a dream, very vivid and compelling, but still a dream.

He was standing in the midst of a forest, alone. Only the moon provided light, slicing through openings in the overhead branches. There were voices all around him, and other sounds.

He started walking, and then he *felt* something. That was the only way to describe the sensation. Perhaps he heard it, too, but it was more like feeling—a feeling of something running toward him.

He turned and looked behind him. In the distance he saw a shape, quite awful, coming at a gallop. He ran so hard that he thought he might collapse, his heart giving way from the strain. He tripped, fell, then stood again. His eyes widened. There was no more forest.

Do not run in fear.

The voice touched his very soul. He reached out, into fog so thick that his hand disappeared just inches from his face. Suddenly he realized there was no ground beneath his feet!

"And yet I am not falling," he heard himself say.

I am holding you in the palm of My hand, beloved friend.

"Where are You?" he asked. "I cannot see You."

Soon, Brian Loeffler. Soon you will see, and know.

Suddenly he saw, though not clearly, just beyond the fog, a man's face—a familiar face with dark skin and piercing eyes. The man held a weapon of some kind.

I have touched his soul, his longing and bitterness, and he is now Mine. You entered his world as My instrument, and he will be with you soon.

Long hair. Dark skin. Piercing eyes.

Something was slung over his shoulder.

The man was reaching for it.

A second passed. No more.

And then the sound of—

An arrow just a fraction of an inch past his head, its feathery end touching his cheek, then lost in the fog surrounding him.

Brian felt no fear, only extraordinary peace.

That is as it should be, Brian Loeffler.

16

Loeffler awoke to a persistent tapping sound. Disoriented and drowsy, he got up from the bed as the door swung open.

A little boy stood in the doorway.

"Come with me," he said in a voice that was barely audible.

He was dressed in a black togalike outfit, its neck and sleeves ringed in gold beaded material.

"Dinner," the boy said when Loeffler hesitated.

Loeffler followed him down the hallway. The guard at the end stepped aside, and Loeffler could tell that he was following them.

Loeffler and the little boy walked across the artificial

main street to a building that looked like a mess hall. It turned out to be quite large inside, with hundreds of folding chairs and people who stopped talking when they entered.

At the far end, on a raised platform, Marconi, the senator, and several others sat at a long covered table.

"Join us for dinner!" Marconi's voice came over the loudspeaker.

Loeffler was about to say no when he saw a round metal covered cart being wheeled into the large room by a good-looking teenage boy.

Marconi stood.

"You operate in your safe and sane world and cast judgment on any other! You hold your Bible out as the only volume of wisdom from heaven. Don't forget, Lucifer came from there also."

He held up a black leather book, the words *Satanic Testament* clearly printed in gold on its cover.

"The only bible that matters!"

He rested it back on the table and bowed his head, everyone else except Loeffler following his lead.

"Lord of Darkness, king of the Black Pits, we honor thee now with this feast of which we are about to partake."

And then he sat down.

The teenager rolled the cover back.

"Sir?" he asked. "The usual?"

"The usual."

Loeffler took one look at the contents of the cart before he started screaming. He turned, pushing the youngster aside, heading for the front entrance.

"It's been locked," Marconi shouted at him. "You *have* to stay."

Loeffler felt something hard hit the back of his head before darkness overcame him.

When he regained consciousness, his hands and feet had been bound, and he was sitting in a chair to one side of the podium.

"Ah, you're awake," Marconi said. "You slept through dinner."

"You're sick monsters—all of you!" he screamed.

At some signal, the gathered children arose and started to file out of the building until only Loeffler, Marconi, the senator, and the two other men at the table remained.

"We're going to tell you some very private things," Marconi said, standing and pacing. "You'll go to your grave with knowledge only a privileged few out of two hundred million Americans have at present."

Marconi turned to the senator.

"This is Senator Mark Lambert," he said. "Why don't you fill the reverend in on some of the details?"

Lambert stood and approached the minister.

"Some men go into politics to serve the public," he said sarcastically. "Others do it for another reason—

power. The real power comes not from government alone. There is another source."

"Satan!" Loeffler interjected.

"Satan, yes. With Lucifer's power brought into the governmental arena, there is no end to what can be accomplished. There are different kinds of power, you know."

He grinned broadly.

"And different ways of exerting that power," he added. "For example, we keep the street gangs tied to us because we provide them with guns."

"And it's not only guns," Marconi interjected. "We have some excellent drug connections, too."

"And sex also has something to do with it," Lambert went on. "We provide flesh for the satisfaction of any desire."

Loeffler shook his head.

"You're sick—perverse!"

"Then why doesn't He strike me dead if I am so perverse, if I am such a stench in His nostrils?"

"How do you know He won't?"

"Because the one I follow will protect me."

Lambert bent over, his face only a few inches from Loeffler's.

"How many members of your denomination are serving Satan? If God were so wonderful, why would they turn away from Him?"

"Because they have that choice. Because emotions and intellect are fallible."

"Because Satan is going to be the victor!" Lambert interrupted.

"Not according to God's Word!"

"This is what you are referring to?"

Lambert turned back to the table and reached under it, bringing out a Bible.

"Yes!" Loeffler exclaimed. "The source of all truth!"

Lambert took the Bible and tore whole handfuls of pages out of the binding, scattering them on the ground.

"That's what I think of that musty old book!" he yelled, his face flushed. "My master gives me *all* my needs."

The senator stalked out of the building after smirking at Loeffler.

That left Marconi and his two bodyguards alone with the minister.

"Why are you so dedicated to unraveling what we're trying to accomplish?" Marconi asked. "Tell me. I do want to know."

"Because what you are attempting is wrong—evil."

"By whose standards?"

"By the standards of Christian and secular society."

"But we come from the secular, as you know."

"Why don't you walk up to the average atheist and ask if he considers kidnapping children and subjecting them to ritual abuse an acceptable course of action!"

Marconi snorted.

"Atheists are stupid. They claim to believe in nothing. At least we Satanists have someone to believe in."

"I wonder if having faith in a monster should be considered better than having no belief at all."

"According to your Bible, we all end up in hell anyway. No, admit it, Reverend Brian Loeffler, isn't that the case?"

Marconi shivered slightly, a movement the minister noticed and took advantage of.

"The idea of burning for eternity terrifies you, doesn't it?" Loeffler asked knowingly.

Marconi looked at him, obviously trying to show no emotion.

"Why do you think we try so hard to ensure that Satan is victorious? Your merciful, loving God is driving us to do everything that He apparently finds so abhorrent."

"But the actions preceded the punishment, as far back as Adam and Eve."

"Not that serpent-in-Eden routine!"

"Oh, yes, that routine!"

"Enough!" Marconi said. "Take the reverend back to his room. Our ceremony begins at midnight."

The ceremony was held in the large cavern.

The odor! Loeffler noticed it right away—stale and sweaty and—

His arms were held by two of Marconi's henchmen,

and he was walked from the hotel to the cavern. The odor had been apparent from far away.

Once inside, he saw hundreds of candles around the circumference of the cavern, and scores of people—men, women, and children—all dressed in black togas.

In the middle was the circle of crosses.

As Loeffler entered, though this was done quietly, all seemed to sense his presence, as had been the case at the hall earlier, and turned toward him.

But they seemed different this time, their expressions darker, their eyes narrowed, staring at him, a number of them licking their lips.

He was led down a center aisle slightly to the right of the crosses and on to the opposite end of the cavern.

Waiting there were Mayor Marconi, Senator Lambert, and others he did not recognize.

"Welcome," Marconi said. "Be a spectator, for a while, anyway."

Loeffler was forced to sit down on a folding chair to the right of Marconi and Lambert. He looked out over those gathered in the cavern. He saw faces that were cold, somber, with dark circles under the eyes, faces that were thin and pale. His eyes drifted to the entrance to the cavern.

Something was moving there. He couldn't make out what it was at first, then he saw several figures being led inside, each blindfolded. They stopped in front of the crosses.

"We have come tonight to drink the wine of perdition," Lambert was saying as the people listened intently. "We have come to imitate the sacrifice of the enemy of our great master."

He glowered as he spit out the next words.

"It is written in prophecy that we are come to deceive and destroy, if it were possible, even the very elect of God."

Lambert paused for effect, then added, "Well, my fellow worshipers of the Prince of Darkness, nearly a decade ago, our predecessors gathered in a spot similar to this one. A master plan was worked out. Now our beloved Michael is suffering. "He is dying in prison."

The crowd went nearly berserk then, screaming outrage, fists pounding at the air, clothes being rent, and strange tongues being spoken.

Loeffler recognized one of those tongues! He struggled to his feet and called out to those who spoke, in their own language.

They lapsed into immediate silence, and Loeffler continued speaking.

Several of those in the crowd fell to their knees, sobbing.

Marconi strode over to the minister.

"Stop it!" he demanded.

Loeffler turned to him, tears streaming down his cheeks.

"Your people abuse the gift," he shot back, "but that does not invalidate the genuine expression of something given to us by God Himself. Before the manifestation of truth, any counterfeit from the Devil collapses in its impotence!"

"What did you say to them?"

"That no matter what they've done, God's forgiveness will never be withheld, that it is always there if they but accept His Beloved Son as their Savior and Lord."

Marconi slapped him so hard that Loeffler was knocked onto his back.

One of the men who had fallen to his knees now stood and approached the mayor.

"Sir, there *is* something other than hatred, blasphemy, and damnation."

Marconi's bodyguards immediately beat the man into silence. The others who had been reached by Loeffler in that brief moment began to protest.

"Destroy them!" Marconi commanded. "Destroy every one of them!"

And that is what the crowd did to a handful of its own, with such violence that Loeffler could only retch at the sight of the beating, kicking, and clubbing. And when it was over, five bodies were lying at their feet. One, a woman, had said only a single name before they set upon her, though the sound of it made them hesitate a moment: "Jesus."

Marconi was beaming.

"Wonderful! Wonderful!" he said, looking and

sounding like a degenerate orchestra leader bowing before an admiring audience. "And now the reason we gather here tonight!"

He raised his hands.

"The crosses!" he shouted. "Time to adorn the crosses!"

17

Loeffler turned his attention to the captives in the front, one of them a girl he immediately recognized as Rob's friend Laurie. He could hardly forget what she looked like, having shown her picture to scores of people in the process of searching for her. A man he didn't recognize followed Laurie, then someone who seemed somehow familiar to him. An Indian—probably River Brooks. There was Lane Connelly—supposedly dead of his injuries. And finally another young girl. He couldn't be positive, but he suspected it was Becky McClane.

Loeffler struggled to his feet again. There were six crosses, and he knew the sixth was for him!

"Rob, I love you," Laurie called out as she was nailed to a cross.

Tears streamed down her cheeks.

"Dear Jesus, I accept You as my Lord, my Savior," she whispered. "Dear Savior, take my hand!"

Somehow Loeffler managed to work his own hands free of their bonds, adrenaline and the cries of the victims infusing him with strength. Marconi was still on the platform. Lambert had personally taken up a hammer and was nailing River Brooks to one of the crosses. Loeffler dashed up to him, knocking the hammer out of his hand, and the two struggled.

Loeffler broke free and hit the other man squarely in the jaw. Lambert fell flat on his back. Loeffler found a rock and straddled the senator, raising it above his forehead.

"Go ahead!" Lambert yelled. "Go ahead! End my misery."

Loeffler hesitated, looking at the rock, then at the senator, realizing the act he was about to commit. Suddenly he felt a sharp pain in his stomach. Lambert had grabbed a large nail and jabbed it upward into his midsection. Loeffler fell back.

The senator got to his feet, laughing.

"Where's your blessed Savior now?" he mocked. "Where's the One who's supposed to be your guardian, your—"

Without warning, the senator went through a singular convulsion, moving spasmodically, like a stringed puppet gone wild. Turning around, his face filled with fright and pain, he fell inches from Loeffler, an arrow sticking out of his back!

Then he heard Adrian Marconi screaming and saw the mayor stumble forward, an arrow through his neck.

Everyone else panicked. They started running toward the cavern's entrance and into the tunnels leading out from the back.

Loeffler was knocked to the ground; his vision wavered. As the crowd went wild, he saw Dr. Barnett die, crushed beneath their feet.

Seconds later, Loeffler knew something very clearly: that he, too, was dying.

He saw a figure wavering in his sight, standing before one of the crosses, looking up, and sobbing, "My son! My son!"

And he heard a fading voice, barely discernible: "Father. I love you."

And then nothing more.

The figure turned toward him, moving slowly, bending down beside him, reaching out, hoisting him gently, carrying him.

Just then the ground began to shake in one long, awful tremor. Rocks were falling. People were screaming.

Once outside, Loeffler caught a glimpse of the stars.

From the sky came a sudden, encompassing stream of light. And close by, the sound of angels, accompanied by heralding trumpets, angel wings beating through the chill night air.

Henry Running Stream dragged Loeffler as far as he could, just before the whole world was filled with light. The minister was only seconds from death. Running Stream rested the man's head on his lap. "Is this the mouth of hell?" he asked out loud, his head tilted toward the sky, which was now alternating shades of crimson and scarlet.

The answer came soon enough. He saw an enormous beast with wings and a devil's head and ugly, cankered skin. It was surrounded by pure-white beings and desperately trying to get past the circle they formed. None of them was as large as it, but there were vast numbers of them.

"It's happening now," he said excitedly. "Look, Brian Loeffler, *look!*"

There was no response.

"You are so peaceful," Running Stream said. "How can you be so peaceful?"

The Indian looked back at the sky and saw something else. The huge beast was alone now, the other beings gone. It bellowed exaltedly until a figure appeared, clothed in raiment so white, so pure, that it was nearly blinding.

Running Stream saw an amazing encounter then, one that was barely more than a minute in duration but changed his life for time and eternity. He could see the figure's face, a face filled not with rage or vengeance but pity and tears that glistened as they trickled down the shining cheeks. And he heard a voice he could never,

never forget: *Prince of Darkness, you have been defeated!*

The beast roared with fleeting defiance.

Go from this place! the radiant figure said.

Suddenly the beast reached out toward that figure. Its countenance changed briefly into that of a dazzling being, a being far more beautiful than those which had previously surrounded it.

No longer, Lucifer, the figure said in the saddest tone of all. *That can never be again.*

The beast was once again a rotting, repellent hulk. It roared in a cry of such anguish and sorrow that Running Stream found himself driven to tears.

Go! the figure said. *You have done your work. The results of it are at your feet even now. We meet again on the field of blood.*

The beast was gone but the figure remained, turning in Henry Running Stream's direction.

"I have worshiped devils," the Indian said. "Surely I am not worthy."

The figure smiled the most radiant smile he had ever seen, and suddenly Running Stream noticed that those who had died on the crosses back in the cavern were standing by the side of the figure.

"My son!" Running Stream shouted, in the most profound joy he had ever experienced. He stood, reaching both hands toward the sky, palms tilted upward.

And then it was over, but not before words reached his ears just as unconsciousness swept over him: *I love you, Dad. I really love you!*

*   *   *

The epicenter of the earthquake had been off the coast of Santa Monica. It was of the tectonic variety, far below the Pacific Ocean's surface, and registered nearly 6 on the Richter scale.

Man's carefully constructed civilization would be, in a matter of seconds, reduced to pathetic bits and pieces. Yes, there would be a phoenixlike emergence from the debris; yes, people somehow would survive. But many others would die; countless numbers of them would live with psychological scars for many years hence.

But this quake was different from those that had occurred in the Southern California region at various times over the years. It was accompanied by another extraordinary event: From the sky came a blazing shower of flame.

Some thought it a never-before-seen variety of lightning. Others had a theory about some form of kinetic energy caused by forces involved in the quake itself. It hit in only one section of the Santa Monica Mountains.

"Nowhere else!" exclaimed a scientist going over the details a short while afterward.

Others in the conference room voiced their own astonishment.

"It was a region less than a mile square," the first man continued. "Everything in it was burned to a crisp."

Hours later, some strange bits and pieces began to fall into place. One of the oddest was the fact that the state police stations in the Hollywood area responded erratically—in some regions, they did a great deal to help, to keep order; in others, they did little or nothing to respond to the emergency. Nor was the story different with the local police. Law enforcement squads had to be called in from San Diego and northern California.

One by one, hundreds of police, state as well as local, were found dead near their motorcycles or in their cars or in the various stations, or elsewhere. Others died before they could be given professional medical care. Some spoke mysteriously of white doves, not where these came from or what they did, but just that there were thousands of them, so many that they blotted out the sun at one point.

But it was what one officer in particular said, in his final moments of life, that raised the greatest alarm.

"We were controlled . . . by them, by Marconi, by his demons," he blurted out, agony in his voice. "Threats . . . drugs . . . money . . . everything they could . . . throw . . . at us. And they won."

Troopers from Fresno, California, acting upon reports they had received from a variety of sources, searched out the exact location of that unprecedented display of celestial fire. They found buildings that were nothing more than blackened shells and mounds of ashes with human bones scattered among them.

"A holocaust!" one of the troopers exclaimed.

As he stood in the midst of the devastation, he seemed to remember something.

"It's happened before," he said, scratching his head.

"Not here," his partner remarked.

"No . . . in Kansas somewhere, a place called Providence Junction, I think."

"Oh, yeah . . ." the partner said, remembering as well.

Several troopers stumbled out of a cave entrance a few hundred yards ahead, their helmets in their hands.

They were hardly able to stand.

"You don't want to see," one of them stuttered, his face drained of color.

What they had been confronted with was a very large cavern with hundreds of bodies inside.

"It was like a scene out of hell," one trooper said. "Little fires are still burning in there!"

"Man, what was it like when the flames were really raging?" another asked.

Minutes later, they found the only two survivors. Huddling behind some rocks at the western edge of the site were a girl named Becky and an Indian named Henry Running Stream.

18

Plenteous grace with thee is found,
Grace to cover all my sin;
Let the healing streams abound,
Make and keep me pure within.

Charles Wesley

Within hours, at Four Gospels Christian College, the mess precipitated by the quake was in the process of being cleaned up. Every building had been constructed with the potential of such a calamity in mind. There was damage, but structurally the buildings were in astonishingly good shape.

Judson McClane was in his office, listening to radio reports of damage elsewhere: the Los Angeles Civic

Center; the Hollywood Bowl; building after building!

Lord, thank You, he said in silent prayer, *thank You for sparing us.*

Not everyone was as fortunate. Many homes had been seriously affected; cars had run into fissures that had opened up on at least one of the freeways; electrical lines were down; phone service was erratic.

"Some buildings have been completely destroyed," the newscaster was saying. Several were listed, including the sanitarium to which Becky had been committed.

Becky! My Becky!

He started a series of if onlys. If only he had been more aware of how she was hurting; if only her mother hadn't died; if only they hadn't moved to California. None of that would change the situation. Becky was gone!

He heard a knock at the door.

"Come in," he said, his voice cracking with emotion. It was Charlotte.

"I thought I heard you, Judson," she said, smiling. "Everything seems to be under control as far as the quake damage is concerned. There was so little!"

McClane got to his feet and told her the sanitarium had been completely destroyed, catching her as she fell into his arms. In a minute, she pulled away from him, looking deeply into his eyes. "Judson, it's quite strange," she said.

"What is, my love?"

"I feel the strangest sort of peace. How could I feel that way now?"

He shook his head, putting his arms around her again, the two of them standing there like that, not speaking, just holding each other.

Later they decided to go outside and get some fresh air. The sky was clear, the air carrying more than a hint of the nearby Pacific Ocean.

Rob Walker and Corey Alderton were just ahead on the lawn, both on their knees in prayer.

As the McClanes walked past, they could hear a little of what the two were praying about.

"Laurie's probably dead, Lord," Rob was saying. "I pray that she's with You now."

The McClanes stopped and knelt on the grass next to the two young men. Charlotte waited for a moment of silence and then started her own petition, a prayer that was very much like Rob's. In a short while, the four of them joined hands and went on praying in rotation.

Later that evening, there was a chapel service.

All the students attended, along with every staff member.

Judson McClane stood before them at the podium in front of the large, circular auditorium. Only one of the large stained-glass windows had been damaged by the quake.

"We have come through quite a calamity," he was saying. "We have come through whole, physically as well as spiritually."

"Sir!" one male student stood and called out. "We came through, yes, because of the Lord but also because of you, sir."

Everyone in the auditorium stood and gave McClane a sustained ovation.

He couldn't help himself as the tears started to flow.

They started singing "Abide With Me," the rich sounds of the old hymn filling the auditorium.

No one noticed when the double doors at the back opened wide and two figures came in.

They looked at each other, and the girl smiled.

"God bless you," she said, meaning each of those three words more than ever before in her life.

And then she turned toward the front.

Judson McClane noticed his daughter almost as soon as she stepped inside and joined his wife as she ran down the center aisle. Becky McClane, quite weak from her ordeal and barely able to move, waited for them, her arms open wide.

They lost themselves in their rejoicing, lost themselves before hundreds of students and staff, not caring about anything but their joy, their relief, their oneness with one another and with the Lord who had brought them together again.

Epilogue

Later, one of the male students discovered a chest of stiffened leather in a corner of the lobby and brought it to McClane.

"Sir, I found this a few minutes ago," the young man told him.

"Do you know what's inside?" McClane inquired.

"No, sir, I don't."

The student cleared his throat nervously.

"I thought it would be improper to poke around."

McClane nodded appreciatively.

"Any idea who left it, son?"

"I can't say, sir. I don't know."

McClane stood and walked over to the chest.

"Old leather. Beautiful!" he exclaimed, running his

hand along the sides and over the lid.

Then he opened the chest.

Inside were splintered, broken pieces of wood.

"A lifetime of false gods," McClane remarked, his voice not much above a whisper. He could recognize some of the fragments all too easily. "Destroying what has been in your tribe for generations takes courage."

"I suppose you're right, sir," the student agreed. "We risk the wrath of family and friends when we do it."

"More than that, we *guarantee* that wrath, that rejection. But the Lord honors our act of sacrifice tenfold, if not in this life, then in heaven."

"Sir?" the young man asked.

"Yes, son?"

"In the corner there's a sheet of paper."

McClane saw it and dug it out. As he was reading the contents, in his mind was an image of a poverty-stricken little village, and a lone figure whispering good-bye for the last time.

"What does it say, sir?" the student inquired.

McClane handed the sheet to him.

Seconds later, they were crying together, in an intimate and precious moment, because of words of confession and rebirth that neither would ever forget.

*We look with horror at what is happening in the
world around; it shocks us, as it must if there are
among us any still left with a righteous spirit.
But why should we be so surprised—as we all too
often are—at the reality of Satan in this world-
once-Eden, for all we have to do is consider what
the master of infamy seems willing to attempt in
wretched desperation to forestall the inexorable
judgment of God, which is forever and ever, putting to waste his awful flounderings. . . .*